Alan Hunter was born in Hoveton, Norfolk in 1922. He left school at the age of fourteen to work on his father's farm, spending his spare time sailing on the Norfolk Broads and writing nature notes for the *Eastern Evening News*. He also wrote poetry, some of which was published while he was in the RAF during the Second World War. By 1950, he was running his own book shop in Norwich and in 1955, the first of what would become a series of forty-six George Gently novels was published. He died in 2005, aged eighty-two.

The Inspector George Gently series

Gently to the Summit

Alan Hunter

ROBINSON

Constable & Robinson Ltd
55–56 Russell Square
London WC1B 4HP
www.constablerobinson.com

First published by Cassell & Co., 1961

This paperback edition published by Robinson,
an imprint of Constable & Robinson Ltd, 2011

A copy of the British Library Cataloguing in
Publication Data is available from the British Library

ISBN: 978-1-78033-146-1

Typeset by TW Typesetting, Plymouth, Devon

Printed and bound in the UK

3 5 7 9 10 8 6 4 2

To
ELEANOR ROBSON BELMONT
than whom no irascible author could have
a more painless and talented adaptor;
admiringly, on her accomplishing the
play script of *That Man Gently*

The characters and events in this book are fictitious;
the locale is sketched from life.

CHAPTER ONE

I T WAS A preposterous business.

As Gently remembered it, it began in the silly season, in August, with a small filler paragraph in the *Evening Standard*. There was no way of telling that it would go any further and certainly not that it would ever make the national front page. It read as follows:

COMIN' ROUND THE MOUNTAINS

The annual meeting of the Everest Club – the surviving members of the 1937 expedition – was last night interrupted by an unidentified hoaxer. Forcing his way into the Asterbury Hotel, where the meeting was held, he announced himself as Reginald Kincaid, the climber who lost his life on Everest. He insisted that he had climbed Everest but had come down on the wrong side, and had spent the intervening years in the hands of Tibetan bandits. Club Secretary Dick Overton described the story as 'fabulous'. He added: 'There is no possibility whatever that Kincaid could have survived.'

That was all; an amusing titbit for the Londoner's tea-table, the counterpart of a thousand other crackpot stories. In his official position Gently had to do daily with such people; he could have quoted half a score anecdotes quite as dotty as this one. So he was surprised when, a week later, the matter cropped up again, this time to earn itself a thirty-six-point heading:

COMPANY DIRECTOR SUES KINCAID HOAXER
'Story A Slander,' Says Former Expeditionist

Company Director Arthur Fleece, who led the 1937 Everest Expedition, has instructed his solicitors to sue the man calling himself Reginald Kincaid. He told our reporter: 'The fellow's tale is a slur on Kincaid's memory, besides being a personal slander on myself. It was I who made the final assault with Kincaid, and was the last person ever to see him alive. About fifteen hundred feet below the summit I became exhausted. Kincaid was going strongly and refused to turn back. It was hazardous for one of us to continue alone, but he would not be argued out of it, and I was in no condition to stop him. I managed to stagger down to the assault camp, but Kincaid never returned. The next morning, before we could search for him, the monsoon had broken. There can be no doubt at all that poor Kincaid died on the mountain.'

The man who calls himself Reginald Kincaid is staying in the Beaufort Hotel in Kensington. In a statement to the press he claimed that Fleece separated from him on the mountain, and that he continued the ascent only after searching for his companion. He reached the summit, but in a state of exhaustion and daze. He was unable to remember the route by which he had got there. By mistake he chose the South Col when he began his descent, and fell into the hands of a party of Tibetans who had been tracking a Yeti. He expressed himself as very eager to trace his wife, and asked reporters to print an appeal to her to get in touch with him.

Everest Club Secretary, Dick Overton, asked to comment on 'Kincaid's' story, said that it was a tissue of impossibilities from beginning to end. No man could have made an unaided descent of Everest, especially with monsoon conditions setting in. He estimated that at the summit Kincaid would have had only three hours' supply of oxygen. The account of Tibetans tracking a Yeti was the 'utterest bilge'. The Tibetans regarded the Yeti as being supernatural. To cap it all, the South Col would land Kincaid in Nepal, and any people he ran into would be Nepalese. When asked if any of the Everest Club members recognized 'Kincaid', Overton replied that it was twenty-two years since any of them had set eyes on him.

The report was accompanied by photographs of Fleece and the alleged Kincaid, the former a bald, smooth-faced man, the latter ascetic and rather vague-looking:

there was also a reproduction of a plaque belonging to the Everest Club; it bore the likeness of a square-jawed youth and the inscription: 'Kincaid: First on Everest: 1937'.

The next stage was more predictable. This was Sunday newspaper stuff. The *Sunday Echo* scooped its rivals and printed 'Kincaid's' exclusive story. With banner headlines and dramatic artwork the epic was blasted at the world, the *Sunday Echo* caring nothing about further legal action by Arthur Fleece. And it was a story worth telling, however palpably untrue. Aided by one of the *Echo*'s feature-writers, 'Kincaid' made an exciting job of it. One read of his terrible struggle on the mountain, his capture by ruthless, bloodthirsty bandits, his wanderings up and down Tibet, his flying visit to the Secret City. A little difficulty might have been encountered in winding up this wondrous farrago, but 'Kincaid's' imagination proved quite equal to the task. In a vivid final instalment he told of a massacre by Chinese soldiers, of his escape with a bag of uncut gems and his fearsome crossing of the Himalayas. At Kathmandu he had sold an emerald and expedited his journey to Bombay; there he had sold the remainder of the stones and shipped on the *Kermadec* for Tilbury. The series was sold on the spot for publication in book form, and Arthur Fleece, growing angrier and angrier, talked of damages of transatlantic proportions.

It was at this point, as Gently knew, that the authorities had shown an interest – mildly and apologetically, as though afraid of making fools of themselves. The story was checkable at its latter end and they checked it with care. They also probed about quietly for the true antecedents of 'Kincaid'. Their results were surprising. They supported 'Kincaid' at every point. He could be traced back from Tilbury, to Bombay, to Kathmandu. He had indeed sold some uncut stones and had transferred the money to a London account. And there was no record of his having been in England until he walked off the *Kermadec* at Tilbury.

Gently had mulled it over with Pagram, who'd had a hand in the inquiries. 'So as far as you know he's telling the truth . . . he could really be Kincaid?' 'My dear Gently, what can one think? His tale is true as from January last. And in December, according to the Foreign Office, there *was* a rising in Southern Tibet . . .'

The affair took a different turn when 'Kincaid' went to law himself; not against Fleece but against the *Sunday Echo* in the shape of its editor and feature-writer. They had, he claimed, grossly distorted and misrepresented his account, had taken no notice of his amendments, and had published a version he had never seen. As soon as this suit became known he was seized on by a television sponsor and was 'Given a chance to put his viewpoint' before a panel of three experts. The performance was unedifying; the experts bullied him unmercifully. They produced maps, books, authorities, and a complex table of dates. 'Kincaid', a slim, jerky figure with a gaunt, worried face, was as vague and as incoherent as he had ever looked in the photographs. Yes, he realized that it was a miracle that he had got down off Everest. Yes, he understood that *one* side of the South Col was in Nepal. No, he had been misquoted about the Tibetans tracking a Yeti . . . they worshipped them, you know. They were on a religious mission . . . For most of the half-hour he was made to look very small; but then, unexpectedly, he came near to turning the tables. A native Tibetan was produced who could speak no English, and 'Kincaid' chatted away to him with fluency and animation. His last act, as he saw the programme was about to be faded out, was to turn appealingly to the camera: 'If my wife should be watching this programme . . .'

His wife! His search for her seemed to be genuine, in any case. He was reported to be spending most of his time in the hunt. Advertisements appeared in the personal columns begging her to contact him, and any interview he gave always ended with the same message. And it was a fact that the real Kincaid would have had no other relatives to appeal to. He was an orphan and his guardian had died before the 1937 expedition. But if Mrs Kincaid was alive she gave no indication of being so, nor did anyone come forward who could tell of her whereabouts.

Meanwhile, 'Kincaid' had found a champion among the Everest Club members; one Raymond Heslington, by profession an archaeologist. Heslington claimed that after watching 'Kincaid's' appearance on TV he had been struck by a slight scar which showed above 'Kincaid's' right eye. The original Kincaid had been marked by such a scar. Heslington produced a snapshot which he contended would prove it. The snapshot was published in *The Times*, and a lively controversy arose: the Everest Club divided bitterly over this Question of The Scar. Heslington met Kincaid and put a number of questions to him, and as a result his belief was confirmed and he became a militant crusader. He wrote ferocious letters to the press demanding recognition for 'Kincaid', a knighthood at least, and a pension on the Civil List.

It wasn't often, Gently reflected, that such a brainstorm struck the capital. While it lasted, you could hear arguments about Kincaid everywhere. He was a madness that got into people, goading them to foolish actions; they took Kincaid like an infection and came out in a rash of folly. But it was too hectic to last long, and in a month it was over. Nothing was settled, nothing was done, and *l'affaire* Kincaid began to recede. From being a figure of intense interest and a national curiosity, 'Kincaid' sank back towards the obscurity from which he had so startlingly sprung. His wife was still unfound, his identity remained a mystery, and only the various lawsuits he had provoked kept his ghost before the public. By October, they had forgotten him.

Then:

Another Climber Killed On Snowdon

Once again a short paragraph preceded the avalanche. The report had arrived too late, probably, to be dealt with at length, or else the editor had decided not to stir up dust over it.

Snowdon claimed its third victim in a fortnight today when Arthur Edward Fleece, a company director of London, received fatal injuries following a fall while climbing. A Mountain Rescue Team from Pen-y-Gwryd recovered the body this afternoon. Fleece leaves a widow.

The morning papers expanded this with some interesting additions, though they were still uncertain about giving it importance. At the time of his death Fleece had been on the Everest Club's annual outing, one of which had taken place every year since 1937. The ramble had commenced from the Gorphwysfa Hotel, the members suiting themselves about their paths to the summit. Fleece had chosen the Pyg Track and was one of the first to reach the top. He was seen on the ridge approaching the summit by members on the Pen-y-Pass route. Then, as the others were climbing the Zigzags, a cry was heard from the summit, and a moment later Fleece was seen to fall from the precipices on their left. There were no indications as to how the accident occurred. Another member who had reached the summit was unaware of Fleece's presence there. The papers garnished this account with references to Fleece's part in *l'affaire* Kincaid, but the overall impression Gently received was that they were waiting for a Sign.

It came, twenty-four hours later, vanquishing editorial diffidence. Across the front page rocketed the news:

KINCAID CHARGED WITH MURDER
OF FLEECE

By half-past ten that morning Gently knew he'd
bought the case. The Assistant Commissioner had sent
him a memo desiring a conference at that hour. By a
little probing Gently had ascertained that no other case
of importance had broken, so he was fairly certain of
what was in store when he tapped and entered the
A.C.'s office. As he went in a sharp-eyed plain-clothes
man who had been sitting there, rose politely. The
A.C. beamed at Gently through his tortoiseshell-
framed glasses.

'Morning, Gently. Meet Chief Inspector Evans of
the Caernarvon C.I.D. Evans, this is Superintendent
Gently, one of our principal nutcrackers.'

'I've heard of you, sir.' Evans stuck his hand out
eagerly. He was a man of about forty-five and spoke
with a vibrant Welsh accent. Gently shook the
outstretched hand and nodded to him vaguely; then he
pulled up a chair and sat. Evans too resumed his seat.

'It's the Kincaid business, Gently. As you've probably guessed already.'

'Mmn.' Gently nodded. He fiddled with his pipe.

'We've got our man in the cells at Bow Street. He'll
be transferred tomorrow. But in the meantime the
Chief Inspector has run into a snag.'

'What sort of a snag?'

'You'd better tell him yourself, Evans.'

The Welsh inspector leaned forward. 'It's like this,
sir,' he said. 'If this chummie really is Kincaid, then it's

an open and shut case. But if he isn't – well, then it's just a lot of blind foolishness!'

Gently puffed. 'Isn't that what it's been all along?' he asked.

'I know, man. But there are facts. We couldn't help but have him arrested.'

'So why has he got to be Kincaid?'

'Why, to give him a proper motive. He'll get off as easy as pie unless we can pin him down on that.'

'You've read the papers, have you, Gently?' put in the Assistant Commissioner. 'If so, you must know the story Kincaid has been telling. He as good as said that Fleece abandoned him up there on Everest, which in the circumstances was tantamount to signing his death warrant. There's your motive: revenge. Provided he really is Kincaid. If he isn't, there's only this slander suit for a motive.'

'And it's not enough!' Evans exclaimed. 'We should lose this case for certain. You don't go pushing people off Snowdon merely because of a slander suit.'

Gently hunched, leaning back in his chair. It was running to form, *l'affaire* Kincaid! It worked by a form of chain reaction which led you from one piece of idiocy to another.

'What are the facts, then?' he enquired.

'They are plain as daylight,' retorted Evans. 'If you listen I will go over them in just the order they happened.

'At first it looked like an accident, I don't mind telling you. There was nothing at all to say that Fleece hadn't overbalanced or something. He was a climber,

10

that's certain, and the top of the Wyddfa isn't treacherous, but it might be he walked down to the edge and contrived to lose his footing there. The only thing at all suggestive was that he wasn't quite alone. There was this other fellow, Heslington, who must have been up there when it happened.

'So that made me rather careful when it came to taking statements. Heslington, in particular; I had to go through all his movements. I knew, because I had read it, that he was no friend of the deceased's, and when I put it to him he was frank with me – he didn't like the man at all. Now, just look at this plan.'

Evans produced a folded sheet. It was a sketch map of Snowdon summit and the ridges falling away from it. A small rectangle marked the café which lay niched in below the top, a circle beside it was the cairn, a hatched line the mountain railway. At the side of the café away from the cairn a pencilled cross had been placed, and another at the side of the cairn furthest away from the café.

'Do you see where these tracks come up from the Gorphwysfa? There's the Pyg Track see, it's the shorter of the two. That was Heslington's way and he was the first one to the top. When he'd got to the ridge here, he says, the others were down by the Glaslyn. So there he is, at about one o'clock, just arrived at the summit. What does he do? He decides that he might as well eat his lunch. So he goes round the café, which is closed in October, and sits down out of the wind, where I've put this cross.

'Fleece was behind him on the Pyg Track and he

arrived on top about twenty minutes later. We're asked to assume that he stuck to the track, which passes the café on the left. So like that it's quite possible that Heslington might not have seen him – nor heard him, neither, when he went over the edge. This other cross by the cairn marks the spot from which he fell.

'When that happened the rest of the party were climbing the Zigzags to the ridge. Overton, the secretary, was nearest to the top. He had the sense to take the time – it was one twenty-five – and he called down to the others to make an attempt to reach the body. Then he hurried up the Zigzags and along the ridge to the summit, where he came upon Heslington still eating his lunch. He didn't waste time on him, but went and broke into the café, and from there he phoned down to Llanberis for the Mountain Rescue Team.'

Evans paused to lick his lips. 'So far so good. But then we heard something from Heslington which gave the business a different look. While he was sitting beside the café he'd seen a third party about there, a man wearing a brown tweed jacket and a pair of grey slacks. Only a glimpse of him he'd caught, just as the man was going away from him: he was on the railway track, here, and running down it like the devil. And this is the interesting part. He puts the time at one-thirty. Which is five minutes, look you, after Fleece took his tumble.

'As you can imagine, I went over the ground with a magnifying glass, but it's mostly bare rock and there was nothing for me to find. A bit of shale was kicked out where I've put the cross, only that told us nothing one way or the other. It was one of my constables who showed the best sense – he climbed up the cairn and had a poke around there. And he spotted this small item.' Evans dived his hand into his pocket. 'When you see it, you will think we were a little slow in drawing conclusions.'

He produced a silver cigarette-case and handed it to Gently. It was of silver, a tubby design which had fallen from favour years earlier. A florid pattern was engraved on it though this was wearing thin, but on an oval plaque in the centre appeared clearly the monogram: RTK. Pasted down inside it was a faded snapshot of a climber.

'Did you find any latents on it?'

Gently passed it to the Assistant Commissioner.

'No; it was smeary.'

'It's a poor surface for prints. Was there anything inside it?'

'A couple of Churchman's No. 1. And we found one he'd lit and thrown away, about a couple of feet distant.'

'You examined them, of course?'

'Oh yes, you bet I did! But there were only smears on them, and just the edges of prints.'

Gently nodded. He puffed several times without speaking. Chummie had lit a cigarette . . . thrown it away . . . dropped his case. And his hands would seem to have been sweating on that cool October mountain. It made an interesting picture: he filed it away in his mind.

Evans continued: 'You'll say I was dumb not to have connected the case with Kincaid, but when we found it Kincaid hadn't been mentioned in the business. I showed it to Overton and Heslington and the rest of the party, and none of them admitted having seen it before. Then Overton rang me from his hotel; he wanted to have the initials again. When I gave them to him he told me that they were the same as Kincaid's. I got them to look at the case again, especially the snapshot inside it, but none of them would commit themselves to a positive identification.

'But now, with Kincaid's name brought in, we could begin to see daylight. The next step was to inquire whether he'd been seen in the district. And you know how it is once you've got the right lead – people tumble over themselves to give you a helping hand. I got a call from Llanberis to say a young man had been in there. On the day of the crime he'd stopped at Llanberis and had coffee at the Snowdon Café. While he was having it he saw another customer who looked like the pictures of Kincaid, and since we were investigating Fleece's accident he thought we might like to know.

'That started it. I went to Llanberis directly. In a couple of hours we had Kincaid properly taped. He'd been making inquiries about his wife – that's the story he tells, anyway – and he'd given his name and some particulars at a boarding-house he'd inquired at. Then he was remembered at the Snowdon Café, where they packed him some sandwiches, and was seen heading up the street towards where the Llanberis track begins. To

14

round it off he returned at four and took a local hire-car back to Caernarvon. He was dropped at the Bangor Hotel, where he had booked for two nights.'

Gently asked: 'Did anyone notice how he was dressed?'

'Oh yes. He was wearing a tweed jacket and slacks.'

'The same as Heslington described?'

'Well . . . the slacks must have been lovat. But he had on a brown jacket, and I found the clothes at his hotel here.'

'What's his story?'

'He admits he was there all right. Couldn't very well deny it, in the face of the evidence. I came up here yesterday as fast as I could, and I had a long talk with him down at Bow Street Station.'

'Where did he say he went?'

'Not up Snowdon, you can bet your life! No, a nice lonely scramble up to the Devil's Kitchen. I've given Llanberis a tinkle to have them check his story. There might have been climbers from Ogwen who can give him the lie.'

'So you've no independent testimony to show he actually climbed Snowdon?'

'Wait a minute!' Evans ventured a wink. 'You're getting along too fast. Of course, I made some inquiries at the bottom of the track, and I've two witnesses who saw someone like him going up at about half-past ten.'

'Would that fit in?'

'It couldn't be better for us. Like that he would arrive there around twenty minutes before Heslington.'

'How good is the identification?'

15

'Well, I admit it might be stronger. They only saw him through their windows, and the houses stand back, like. But then I've a separate witness who saw him coming down again. There isn't much doubt, man. I had to charge him on the facts.'

'Mmn.' Gently scratched a match. 'And you showed him the cigarette-case?'

'Of course. And it shook him. He pretended he couldn't remember it.'

'Is that snapshot anything like him?'

'It might have been him at one time. They're going to blow it up for me and try a superimposing job.'

The Assistant Commissioner removed his glasses and gave them a polish with a handkerchief. He beamed from one to the other. 'So now you see, Gently,' he said. 'As long as Kincaid is Kincaid we've got a good fighting case; but if he isn't, then our best evidence is tantamount to irrelevant. It doesn't matter that we can show he was up that mountain. It doesn't matter that we can show he was standing on the cairn. We've got to show that he had a motive for shoving Fleece over the edge, otherwise his defence can write it off as an accident.'

Gently reached for the cigarette-case. 'This is a paradox in itself, of course . . .

'How do you mean, Gently?' The Assistant Commissioner shot him a quick look.

'Well . . . if Kincaid isn't Kincaid, how did he come by this case? And if Kincaid is Kincaid, where did *he* get it from?'

The A.C. swung his glasses for a moment. Then he

said: 'Yes . . . I take your point. The first involves us in a wild coincidence; the second in a wild improbability. It's difficult to believe that a mere hoaxer could have acquired the case, and even more difficult to believe that Kincaid would still possess it. In the first place he would hardly have taken it with him up Everest. It's solid silver and weighty. He'd have left it behind.'

'Just so.' Gently took a sight down his pipe at the trinket. 'And that leaves the situation rather open, don't you agree? He left it behind – a likely souvenir for some other member of the party. And they were each and all of them on Snowdon when, or soon after, Fleece got the push.'

Evans flushed like a turkey-cock, his eyes growing rounder. 'My God!' he exclaimed. 'What a stupid fellow I am! I never looked at it that way . . .'

'There could be some explanation.'

'No man – you've hit it. You've hit the nail on the head!'

'Hold it, everyone.' The A.C.'s voice came drily. 'Let's try to preserve our sense of proportion about this.' He went on polishing his glasses, finally setting them back on his nose. He said to Evans: 'Now you know why we're all so fond of Gently!'

'But it's true, sir,' Evans blurted. 'You have only to consider—'

'It's true that, as usual, Gently has holed a neat case. But he hasn't knocked it down, Evans, so don't despond yet. A little routine investigation may stop the hole up again. And, Gently, that's just what I've called you in to do: a little routine investigation into the

17

antecedents of Kincaid. I've spoken to the Public Prosecutor about it and you were the man he asked to have assigned – so there you are: that's the job. You're to give us Kincaid's identity on a platter.'

Gently stirred his feet disapprovingly.

'Hasn't some investigation been done?'

'Yes.' The Assistant Commissioner picked up a file which had been lying in his 'Action' tray. 'Here you are, for what it's worth. It traces Kincaid back to Kathmandu. It says also that the house he lived in was blitzed and so, too, was the registry office where he was married. And we drew a blank with the Press files.'

'In fact, it bristles with leads.'

The Assistant Commissioner grinned impishly. 'For your sake, I hope this doesn't involve another ascent of Everest. But at least you'd have a reason, unlike these queer types who do it. I've often wondered what it is, Gently, that makes an Everesteer tick.'

His grin broadened and he added:

'But what a draw it would be for tourists! For the price of a bomb, one could run a funicular up Everest.'

CHAPTER TWO

G ENTLY TOOK EVANS down to the canteen and bought him a consoling cup of coffee. In spite of the A.C.'s careful handling, the Welsh inspector was down in the dumps. He'd sat in silence in Gently's office while the latter had read through the Kincaid file, then he'd answered a few random questions. But his attention had plainly been wandering.

'It just goes to show, man . . .'

Now he was moping over his coffee, the red flush still clinging to his straight, smooth-skinned features. He was in his forties, but he looked boyish, his hair and eyebrows being fair. He was tall and hard-framed: an ex-rugby-player, probably.

'We don't see much excitement in Caernarvon, look you. I had visions of making myself on a case like this. And it all went so easy, that was the whole trouble about it. One thing led to another . . . I got too cocky, by far.'

'You won't be the first to have bought stock off Kincaid.'

19

'I know, man. I should have gone like a cat on hot bricks. I should have waited till my head cleared before slapping a charge on him, but it's too late now. I've dropped a most almighty clanger.'

'I wouldn't swear to that yet . . .'

'Oh yes. I can sense it. The Assistant Commissioner was very decent, but he didn't fool me, man.'

'But he's right about one thing – there's still a case to be answered. So we'd better have a chat with Kincaid and see if we can chase up an angle.'

In the courtyard a squad car was waiting to take them to Bow Street. It was a drizzling October morning and the Strand had a drear and slatternly look. Umbrellas were bobbing along the pavements, newsboys huddled into doorways, a sky of motionless grey wrack pressed low over pencilled buildings. At the first tobacconist's shop Gently stopped to make a purchase. He returned, to Evans's surprise, with cigarettes of three different brands.

'You do smoke cigarettes, don't you?'

He took charge of Evans's cigarette-case, adding samples from his three packets to the Players already contained in it. Then he handed back the case.

'I've put the Churchmans on the right . . . it's a silly trick, really. But then, we're on a silly case . . .'

At Bow Street Police Court a couple of pressmen stood waiting on the steps and they snapped into action when they saw Gently arrive with Evans. A flash-bulb hissed momentarily, a notebook was thrust under Gently's nose.

'Is it the Kincaid job, Super . . . ?'

'Have there been some developments . . . ?'

He pushed past them into the police station, murmuring something about routine.

Inside the station smelt dank, as though the drizzle had seeped into it. Gently explained his errand at the desk and was passed through to the office. The inspector in charge, who knew Gently very well, shrugged and made a face when Kincaid's name was mentioned.

'I've got a feeling about him, Super . . . you know the sort of feeling?' He gave an expressive nod to make his meaning the more emphatic.

Then Kincaid was fetched in. He was thinner even than the pictures showed him, a spindly, emaciated man whose clothes hung slackly about him. He had a long, narrow skull, a high forehead and a straight nose, his cheekbones were over-prominent and his brown eyes large and intense. He had a small, thin-lipped mouth set in a pessimistic droop. His cheeks were sunken, his hair short and grey. He looked ten years older than the forty-seven he should have been and one placed him directly: a fanatic or a humbug. He had the fey, alien quality of one born to be notorious.

Evans introduced the session.

'This is Superintendent Gently, Kincaid. He has one or two questions he wants to ask you.'

Kincaid fastened his brown eyes on Gently for a moment, then he looked round for a chair and sat down without speaking. Gently perched informally on the office desk.

'Do you smoke, Kincaid?'

'Yes, I smoke.'

His voice was pitched high and he spoke with care. Evans, cued in, offered his case to Kincaid; then he glanced towards Gently with a scarcely perceptible nod. After hesitating, Kincaid had chosen a Churchman.

'Now Kincaid.' Gently waited for the cigarette to be lit. 'I'm rather interested in these inquiries you've been making about your wife. You've had plenty of time to find her, and you've had a lot of publicity. If she was still alive, don't you think she would have come forward?'

The brown eyes stared through the cigarette smoke, but Kincaid made no offer to answer. He sat perfectly still, his disengaged hand resting lightly on his knee.

'You understand me, Kincaid?'

His head nodded once, slowly. It was set on a scrawny neck which projected stalk-like from his collar.

'Well . . . what's your answer going to be?'

When it came it surprised Gently.

'I'm not obliged to say *anything* when you ask me a question.'

'Now see here, Kincaid—' Evans jumped wrathfully to his feet, but Gently waved him away, signalled for him to sit again. Kincaid's mouth had shut tightly and he watched the Welsh inspector with disdain. His bony hand, now tightly clasped, showed points of white along the knuckles.

Gently said smoothly: 'You're quite in order not to answer questions, and I don't intend to ask any about the crime you are charged with. But if you still claim

22

to be Kincaid I'd like some facts about that. If you've changed your mind, all right. We won't go any further.'

'Why should I have changed my mind?'

It was a difficult question. Either Gently told him the truth or he was paving the way for a judicial reprimand. Since Kincaid was charged he couldn't be interrogated about the murder, and it was sailing close to the wind to treat his identity as a separate subject. Gently weighed his answer with care.

'I think you know that, don't you?'

Kincaid rocked his head again. 'Please don't look on me as an idiot.'

'Right. Then perhaps I can have your decision?'

'I don't have to make one. I *am* Kincaid.'

Gently hesitated. 'You can take advice . . .'

'I certainly shall. But it won't alter the fact.'

'It isn't a fact until it's proved.'

'Oh yes it is. And I'll swear to it in court. I'd sooner swing as Reginald Kincaid than be let off as some impostor.'

His face took on a contemptuous twist: he seemed almost to be enjoying himself. For the first time it occurred to Gently that Kincaid might never get to court . . .

'So in that case you'll be ready to help us to establish your identity?'

'Quite ready. And I'll go further – I'll instruct my lawyer to help you too.'

'Then I'd like to return to the question about your wife.'

23

'And I repeat: I don't have to answer your questions.'

Was he mildly sane even? Gently stared at the large, burning eyes. They never changed expression, he noticed, though the thin features had plenty of eloquence. Two glittering dark orbs, they seemed to live independently; they weren't wholly connected to the intelligence behind them.

'Perhaps you'd like to make a statement, then?'

'Oh yes. I'm used to that. I've done nothing else since I came back from India.'

'About your wife.'

'About anything. My opinions are sought after.'

'I'd like her maiden name and some details of origin.'

'Take a note.'

Kincaid crossed one bony leg with the other; then he folded his arms and gazed vacantly at the wall.

'Maiden name, Paula Blackman. Place of birth, not known. Was living with mother in Fulham when married to R. Kincaid. Height, five feet seven. Age, forty-three years. Colouring . . .' He faltered. 'I don't precisely remember that.'

'Was she brunette?'

'I don't remember!' He frowned reprovingly at Gently, adding scoldingly: 'And it's no use your trying to make me. Now I can remember the dress . . . we went to Wales for our honeymoon . . . her shoes . . . her handbag . . . but some things I can't see. It's only natural, isn't it? It's over twenty years ago.'

'How would you recognize her if you saw her?'

'Stop asking me questions! I shall either tell you or I shan't, but I won't answer questions. And as for how I should recognize her, that's a foolish question anyway: one has a faculty for it. You talk like a bachelor.'

Gently sighed. 'All right! Carry on with your statement.'

Kincaid regarded the wall again. 'Take a note,' he said.

His memory was really surprising in both its commissions and its omissions. It could recall a minute detail and then lapse over something important. Yet there seemed no deliberate pattern, no intention of cunning, and one would almost be prepared to swear that the fluctuations were genuine. And, as one grew used to his eccentricities, Kincaid appeared less abnormal. A personality emerged from behind them, unusual perhaps, but firmly intact.

'I'd like to have a statement about your search for your wife.'

'Take a note. I went to our house in Putney . . .'

Only of course it wasn't there, nor the houses of their neighbours, nor anything the way he'd seen it or known it. A bombed site here, a block of flats there, new people, new names, not a soul who remembered Kincaid.

'I saw an announcement and I went to that Everest Club meeting. I don't care about those people, they're nothing to me at all . . .'

But surely some of them must know what had happened to Mrs Kincaid, and it was to question them that he had gone to the Asterbury that night. And there again he was frustrated. He couldn't convince them of his identity. All he'd got from it was a slander suit and a waggon-load of publicity.

'Still, I thought that when my name was published . . . and it was then I began advertising.'

But never a word reached him from Paula Kincaid.

'Can I have a statement on your reactions?'

'Take a note. I'm sure she's alive. I've known that all along, really . . . up there in Shigatse, and Lhasa. The Tibetans have discovered a system and they can tell about people. I knew a priest in Shigatse, and he gave me lessons.'

'A statement about Wales.'

'Continue note. I got the feeling that she was there . . . can you understand that? Like a Tibetan smells his village when he's lost in strange country. We spent our honeymoon there . . . I taught her to love the mountains. We returned several times, Llanberis, Capel, Caernarvon. So I went. I went to those places. I tried to find where we'd stayed. I even went to the Devil's Kitchen, which was her favourite climb. And all the time I felt she was there, her presence was strong among the mountains . . . but I could find her nowhere, and there was nobody to tell me. Then the feeling went dead and I came back to London.'

Kincaid's voice trembled slightly as he made this recital and his blazing eyes looked brighter, more glittering still. He spoke with a compulsive note of conviction, setting even Evans's mouth agape, while the cynical station inspector gazed pop-eyed at the speaker. Yet Gently had heard that same ring in the stories of accomplished liars. And Kincaid had told stories that would have shamed Baron Munchausen . . .

'A statement about the club members who knew your wife.'

'Take a note. Dick Overton, Ray Heslington, and Arthur Fleece.'

'Fleece? Fleece knew your wife?'

Kincaid sneered. 'I don't answer questions.'

'A statement about Fleece.'

'No, thank you. See my lawyer.'

It was infuriating, and there was nothing that Gently could do about it. If only he'd had Kincaid for just one hour before he was charged! The concatenation of those three names dangled seductively in front of his nose, but there was no way for him immediately to sink his teeth into them. Overton – Heslington – and Arthur Fleece. They had all known Paula Kincaid, and one of them had died . . .

'Heslington believed you were Kincaid. Give me a statement on that.'

'Take a note.' Kincaid's sneer had deepened during Gently's silence. 'Heslington's an idiot, but he's a well-meaning idiot. I never had a scar. That's a wrinkle on my forehead.'

'Continue the statement.'

'About Heslington and my wife? He only met her twice, and he could tell me nothing about her. He lives in Wimbledon, you know, though the line passes Putney. Don't ask me what I mean, because I won't be able to tell you.'

'Continue the statement.'

'Of course. There's Dick Overton. Now he knew her rather better; in fact, he was quite a friend. But he didn't believe I was Kincaid – Dick's intelligence isn't his strong point – so of course *he* told me nothing.' Kincaid paused. 'But you could try him.'

'Continue the statement.'

'End of note. I've no more to tell you about my wife.'

'Hmn.'

Gently studied him, trying to reach some conclusion. In his wide experience of human enigmas, Kincaid bid fair to take the cake. For if he were not Kincaid, what second process could have evolved him? From what strange school of life had such a character graduated?

'Give me a statement about your career.'

'Take a note.'

Kincaid grinned horribly. He too had been doing a little studying, his head tilted back, his expression superior.

'Well?'

'I didn't have a career. It was over by the time I was twenty-five. I lived at Salisbury with my guardian and was educated there at the local grammar school. Afterwards I took a post in the town, and then came up here, to Metropolitan Electric. I married Paula in thirty-five as part of the Jubilee celebrations. And I climbed Everest in thirty-seven. After that, see the *Sunday Echo*.'

'That's the sort of stuff you could have dug up somewhere.'

'I didn't promise you anything else. I've been dead above twenty years.'

'You'll have to do better than that. If you want us to prove your identity.'

'No comment. And I'd like to be getting back to my cell.'

'Just one thing more.' Gently produced the cigarette-case, the one which Evans had found on the cairn. 'You've seen this before, but I'm showing it to you again. Perhaps you've remembered something about it which you didn't tell Inspector Evans.'

Kincaid took the case, a frown appearing as he examined it; he turned it over and over and stared long at the snapshot.

'The initials . . . those are mine. I might have had a case like this. But it's gone . . . I can't place it. I can't place the picture.'

'I think you know the case is yours.'

'No, you're wrong. I'd say if I did.'

'It's the one you took to India.'

'Why should I have done a thing like that? I was smoking a pipe when I went there. I smoked nothing else while I was in Tibet . . .'

'But you're smoking cigarettes now.'

'Oh yes, I began again when I got back to Delhi. But we all smoked pipes on the expedition – it was the thing, you know. We were serious young men.'

'Surely that case is the sort of present your wife might have given you.'

Kincaid stiffened. There was a twitching in the muscles about his eyes. He burst out agitatedly:

'No – I'd remember! I wouldn't forget a thing like that. I've never seen it before, I tell you. Take me back to my cell!'

Gently shrugged and motioned to Evans, who went to the door to fetch the constable. Kincaid got jerkily to his feet and began to shamble out. Then at the door he turned suddenly, and tears were streaming down his face.

'I want her back!' he exclaimed brokenly. 'I want my wife . . . I want Paula back again . . .'

'*Back from whom?*' Gently fired at him, but Kincaid didn't seem to hear. Weeping like a child, he permitted the constable to lead him away down the corridors.

Evans sucked in air and slammed the door shut after them. The station inspector shook his head; he put a finger to his temple.

'The skinny bastard. I could kick him from here to Llanfairfechan!'

Evans was furious; he could hardly persuade himself to sit down.

'Take a note. Take a note. Like he was running a bloody press conference! I ask you, would you have thought he had a murder charge pinned on him?'

Gently gave him a rueful grimace. 'There's Kincaid for you, man,' he replied.

'I know. And to think that it's me who's responsible for it. Now we can't lay a finger on him. "Take a note," he says. It makes you wonder why you ever joined a police force at all!'

'He's screwed, that's what,' observed the station

inspector comfortably. 'You don't have to worry, boy. He's booked for Broadmoor anyway.'

Gently said: 'How does his present behaviour compare with yesterday's?'

'It doesn't,' Evans snorted. 'And for why? Because then I had the drop on him.'

'Would you say he was building it up, then?'

'He doesn't need to build it up!'

Gently shrugged. 'He could be sweating on an insanity plea.'

'Oh . . . I see.' Evans was silent for a moment, eyes glaring at nothing. Then: 'Yess . . . it could be that. It could be that very well.'

'There's another thing too.'

Gently began filling his pipe; slow, squarish-tipped fingers packing the rubbed tawny tobacco.

'"Like a Tibetan smells his village" – you remember that bit? It had me wondering at the time . . . how near do you suppose it was to the facts?'

'What facts do you mean, man?'

'The facts of last Monday. Kincaid's journey to Wales, his being in Llanberis and on Snowdon. It's all very romantic and might be due to E.S.P., but there's a simpler explanation: somebody tipped him off that his wife would be there.'

Evans's hand crashed down on the desk, making the issue ink-pots jump. 'But that's brilliant, man!' he exclaimed. 'That's a bloody brilliant piece of surmising!'

'It suggests a certain sequence. I wouldn't like to go any further.'

31

'But it's brilliant – don't you see? It gives us a whole new angle to work on!'

Gently struck himself a light. 'Go on,' he said. 'You tell me.'

'Why, it's over his wife he murdered Fleece, and not what happened on Everest at all.'

'Unless it was part of the same story.'

'Man, there's no keeping pace with you. You're right – of course you're right: it must all have begun in thirty-seven. Fleece was after Kincaid's wife, which is why that Everest incident happened.'

'And he was still after her in fifty-nine?'

'Of course! And somebody warned Kincaid. And he traced the pair of them to Wales, and took his chance up there on Snowdon. Heslington – he's the man to have warned him, and he was on the spot at the time. I'm telling you, man, you've been inspired. It's making sense of the whole affair.'

Gently drew in a mouthful of smoke and blew the smallest of rings at Evans. 'I'm sorry,' he said. 'But it's doing nothing of the kind.'

'But why? Why not, man?'

'Only ask yourself the question. There are too many things which don't square with the hypothesis. For instance, if Heslington was in it, why did he mention seeing Kincaid? Why was he on the summit at all, when he might have had an alibi with the others?'

'He might not have known what Kincaid would do.'

'Then why did he hedge with what he told us? He'd either spill the lot or nothing, not just enough to make us curious. Then again, there's the cigarette-case –

32

don't tell me that Heslington was the one to drop it! Because if he was, then the moral is plain: we'd better scratch Kincaid and start again.'

'But look, if you rule out Heslington for a moment—'

Gently grinned. 'Then we're left with conjecture. And a crying need for some facts before we worry our brains any further.'

Poor Evans hung his head. 'I'm not so sure . . . it's a fine connection . . .'

'It's an alluring theory, so we won't kill it. Only file it for later reference.'

'Then where do you reckon we go from here?'

'We'll go to the bottom, as usual. We'll start with the firm whom Kincaid last worked for and try to pick up the trail from there.'

Gently hooked up the phone and dialled the Central Office desk. Metropolitan Electric, he was told, still flourished out at Hendon. On the point of ringing off he gave the office a further task:

'Check Kincaid in *Who Was Who* and read me over the entry.'

As he listened a pleased smile crept over his face. He dropped the phone back on its cradle and took a few thoughtful puffs.

Evans asked: 'What did they say, man?'

Gently said: 'What you'd expect. Kincaid's story checks with the book. He gave us nothing fresh at all.'

He blew another couple of rings.

I'm beginning to like this case,' he said. It's what the Americans would call a lulu . . . in Wales, you'd have a different name for it.'

CHAPTER THREE

B Y MIDDAY AN uncertain sun had developed in the London sky, warming the grey flood of the Thames and softly colouring the weight of buildings. It was one of those atmospheric moments which occasionally redeemed the grim metropolis, bringing a sentimental glamour to its meaningless pageant of business and poverty. Gently, who loved and hated London, was glad that it had something to show Evans. He felt oddly responsible towards the latter, as though he were entertaining a country cousin. When they left the station at Bow Street he directed their driver to the Cheshire Cheese; they had grilled trout, and he was naïvely pleased by the commendations of the Welshman. Evans ate silently and intently. He was obviously a man who respected his food.

When the coffee came he sighed and lit a comfortable cigarette. He said:

'I'm enjoying myself in spite of it . . . it's a pleasant way to be losing promotion.'

Gently nodded, stirring his coffee.

'Who have you left in charge at Caernarvon?'

'A Sergeant Williams, a right good man. He'll be checking on Kincaid's alibi this moment.'

'I'd like him to extend his inquiries a little. With special reference to Mrs Kincaid.'

'Oh yes. I was going to suggest it.'

'And Fleece, of course. I'd like to pinpoint his movements.'

They returned to the divisional station before driving to Hendon, and Evans rang his sergeant from there with the current instructions. When he rejoined the car he was wearing a slightly puzzled expression.

'Here's a curious thing that Williams has just told me!'

One of their witnesses had given them a false name and address. The address was in Bangor and was factual enough, but the occupiers knew nothing of a 'Basil Gwynne-Davies'. The falsehood had come to light when the author was sought for to sign a statement.

'What was he witness to?'

'That's the thing which surprises me. He's the young fellow who came forward to tell us about seeing Kincaid in Llanberis. It doesn't matter, of course; it's no longer important. But why did he come forward if he didn't want to be mixed up in it?'

Gently grunted. 'Not from a pure love of justice, I'd say! You told Williams to see if he could find him, did you?'

'Yes, and I think he may. The fellow is obviously a local. He may be an undergraduate from Bangor who was cutting lectures on that day.'

The sun had faded and the drizzle returned by the time they reached Hendon. They discovered Metropolitan Electric in a cul-de-sac near the airport. It was huge: an industrial mammoth filling all one side of its street, its approaches lined with parked cars of which most had a new appearance. Its central block had been rebuilt in the style of the New Towns, a tall, soft-brick building with blue panels between vertical windows. In a courtyard below it stood a Rolls and a Bentley and two Jaguars, while above it trailed a yellow pennon bearing the firm's contracted nomenclature: MET. L. The whole street was pervaded by a regular murmur of industry and from the tall windows of the workshops came occasional bright flashes.

Their driver parked in the courtyard; they went up steps to the main door. Beyond it lay a large reception hall with a softly carpeted floor. An ash-blonde in a black dress was sitting at a varnished sapele-wood counter, and she rose with a touch of hauteur to deal with Gently's inquiry.

'Superintendent Gently, C.I.D. I'd like to have a word with your personnel manager.'

'Er — is it the police?' She seemed slow on the uptake.

'That's correct, miss.'

'Oh, in that case . . . Mr Stanley did say . . .'

Her hand crept involuntarily towards the telephone on the counter and then faltered; she smiled brilliantly, as though to cover an indiscretion.

'Then if you'll please wait a moment . . .'

She tripped out through a door behind the counter,

leaving a delicate perfume of violets to mingle with the odour of new furnishings.

Gently shrugged; surprise was a waste of emotion when you were dealing with *l'affaire* Kincaid. They were expected, that was obvious, though why was beyond all conjecture. After twenty-two years and a world war, what was Kincaid to Metropolitan Electric? He'd been only a unit when he was there, a lowly employee among several thousands . . .

The blonde returned.

'If you'll come this way, please . . . Mr Stanley will see you now.'

'Who's Mr Stanley?'

Her eyes widened. 'Mr Stanley is our managing director.'

They followed her down a corridor lit by a succession of plant windows and watched her tap, very softly, on a grained walnut door. The response was scarcely audible, but she had inclined her head to catch it; immediately she threw open the door and announced:

'Detective Gently, sir.'

They went in. The room was spacious and set out with grained walnut furniture. A buff carpet of ultimate softness extended from one skirting to the other. The two windows were fully screened with featherweight venetian blinds, and when the door closed behind them the hum of the workshops was knifed away. A tall, lion-faced man came forward from his desk to meet them.

'Mr Gently – I didn't catch your rank, I'm afraid.'

He was about sixty years of age and had wavy iron-grey hair, and was dressed in a black suit of a subduedly expensive cut. He smiled, holding out a large, manicured hand.

'Ah yes – superintendent. I believe I've seen your name in the papers. But sit down, gentlemen, and let me hear what I can do for you. We don't often have the pleasure of a visit from the Yard, and when we do we like to offer all the facilities we can.'

Gently chose one of the larger chairs. Evans sat to one side of them. Stanley returned to the desk and drew his trousers before sitting. He put his elbows on the desk and rested his chin on his palms, then he leaned forward towards Gently as though to drink in his every syllable.

'Now, Superintendent,' he said.

Gently cleared his throat prefatorily. 'We're investigating the identity of a . . . certain person,' he replied. 'By his own account he was employed here roughly twenty-two years ago. We'd like to check on that with your records and your personnel manager.'

'I see.' Stanley stared, his heavy brows slightly elevated. 'That's quite a time ago, if I may say so, Superintendent. A number of changes have been made since then and there may be some difficulties. As you are no doubt aware, we employ a large number of people.'

'But you keep records, don't you?'

'Oh yes. Very full ones. Our administrative department is the most highly automated in the industry. But twenty-two years! That's asking rather a lot, you know.

Some of our older files, I seem to remember, went for salvage during the war.'

'Including your personnel records?'

'Well, no, perhaps not those. But since our rebuilding I couldn't be certain where the earlier ones are housed.'

'Where were they housed during the rebuilding?'

'Oh, we moved into the south warehouse.'

'Would that be a good place to look?'

Stanley sank into his palms. 'Perhaps,' he said. 'Hmn.'

Gently knew the symptoms of obstruction when he met them, and this had the appearance of a calculated obstruction. He had no doubt that Stanley knew whom the inquiries concerned, and it was plain that they had been anticipated, and probably prepared for. But to what credible purpose? It seemed like straining to swallow a gnat. After all, the information they sought was harmless enough, surely . . . ?

'So you can't produce any records?'

'Now, I didn't say that, Superintendent. But I thought it only fair to warn you that they might be difficult to come at. It may take us a long time to find them.'

'I can call back tomorrow.'

'No . . . I don't think you fully appreciate the difficulties involved. But I'll help you as much as I can. I'll call in our personnel manager.'

Gently shook his head abruptly. 'It seems hardly worthwhile, does it?'

'I thought you wanted to talk to him?'

'I find I've changed my mind about that. Under the circumstances, I don't believe he can help my inquiries much.'

'Then what . . . ?'

Stanley extended one hand from under his chin. He was doing his best, it seemed to say: he would be cooperative if he could. By way of reply Gently rose and crossed to the other side of the room, where, housed in a walnut bookcase, was an extensive collection of reference books. He took down the copy of *Who Was Who* and returned with it to the desk. Then he leafed through it to a reference, picked up a pencil and marked the page.

'Take a look at this . . . in case you haven't seen it before.'

Stanley stared at him hard before condescending to read the paragraph. Then he gave an exclamation.

'Good Lord! The chappie the stink was about.'

'And you notice something else?'

'Yes, of course. And I'm amazed.'

'Amazed that he worked for this firm, Mr Stanley?'

'I never knew of it until this moment.'

Gently nodded very slowly and behind him Evans shuffled a foot. 'You're a bloody liar, man!' was what the shuffle seemed to convey. Stanley continued to gaze at the entry, his eyebrows pushing up his forehead; then he thrust the book aside and met Gently's eyes firmly.

'Well, Superintendent, you've taught me something by calling here.'

Gently's head continued to nod. 'I'm learning something, too,' he said.

'This happened before my time, of course. I was with Intrics before the merger. But I must say I'm surprised not to have heard about it before.'

'So naturally you didn't know Kincaid?'

'No. I couldn't have done, could I?'

'And in spite of all the publicity he's had you never learned that he was once employed here?'

'I – what do you mean, Superintendent?'

'I'm just considering probabilities.'

Stanley coloured. 'Look here,' he said. 'I'm not so sure I like this.'

Gently went back to his chair. He let his eyes rest on the open book. He said:

'Mr Stanley, you go out of your way to make yourself interesting. First you try to stop me obtaining some apparently innocent information, then you pretend not to have known to what the information related. Don't you think I've got grounds for being a little bit curious?'

'That is perfectly fantastic.'

'I don't think so, Mr Stanley.'

'I deny absolutely having tried to prevent your inquiries!'

Gently gave a faint shrug. 'Then why are we sitting here now? Why wasn't I taken to the personnel manager, who was the man I asked for?'

There was a pause; Stanley shot him a number of most unfriendly looks. He obviously would liked to have flown at Gently and was preventing himself with difficulty. Finally he threw out a couple of 'Tchas!' and stalked across to a cabinet. There he poured himself a whisky, which he tossed back with a sweeping gesture. He returned to the desk.

'All right,' he said. 'I was foxing. I admit it. I knew about Kincaid all along, and I was afraid this would happen.'

'Afraid what would happen, Mr Stanley?'

'Why – you, the press, everything! Do you think I want Met. L dragged into it, and to have it spread all over the papers? It's – it's senseless, that's what it is.' He swept the air with two large hands. 'It's been a scandalous business from start to finish. You take my tip – you hang the fellow.'

'Mmn.' Gently kept watching the book. 'And that's your reason for being uncooperative?'

'Good Lord, what other reason do you want? Should a firm like us be dragged through the mire?'

'You wouldn't be dragged very far, I hope.'

'Quite far enough, when you're doing our scale of business. How do you suppose our customers are going to react to it – Met. L linked with a scandal and a murder? People in America – Europe – Asia: hundreds of thousands of pounds' worth of contracts! Why, the market is as sensitive as a piece of raw flesh. A thing like this could do us incalculable damage.'

'All we want are a few facts about Kincaid's past.'

'A few facts!' Stanley's hands fell chopper-like on the desk. 'And tomorrow, in all the papers, "Murder Hunt at Met. L" – that's what your few facts are going to do to this firm. I ask you, gentlemen, see it my way for a moment! Look at it purely as business, as exports, as wage-packets. You've got your man and presumably you've got a case against him: is it worth what it's going to cost to come scandalmongering here?'

Carried away by his own rhetoric, Stanley went to fetch another drink. He brought it back, sipping it slowly, like a man who felt he'd made his point. Gently's shoulders hunched higher; he angled a glance towards Evans. Further and further did Mr Stanley go out of his way to be interesting . . .

Gently said: 'Did you happen to know Fleece personally?'

Stanley resumed his surprised look. 'Actually, yes. I have met him.'

'Was that recently?'

'Fairly recently. We're in the same line of business. His firm is Electroproducts – domestic appliances, mainly goods for the home market. He's subcontracted once or twice, so I've met him in the way of business.'

'And you know Mrs Fleece?'

The surprise yielded to a frown. 'I think so. In fact, I'm certain. I must have met her at social functions.'

'So you knew the Fleeces socially?'

'Good Lord no! Not in the way you imply. But being in the trade you attend the same functions, and so you meet a lot of people on – what shall I call it? A limited social basis. Now I think of it, I do remember her. She's a rather attractive dark woman.'

'Strong . . . energetic?'

Stanley laughed. 'I couldn't say. But she's the feminine sort of woman. And, as I say, rather fetching.'

'What is Mrs Kincaid's colouring?'

Stanley went completely still. His grey eyes seized

on Gently's, probing, thrusting at the detective's blankness. Then his eyes switched away.

'Of course, I never met either of them.'

'Her name was Paula. Paula Kincaid.'

'I can only repeat that I never met them.'

'But you remember now that Kincaid was employed here?'

'I admitted I did. But dash it, only as a wage clerk.'

'Thank you for the information.' Gently inclined his head politely. 'I didn't know that. But now I do, we'll be getting along to the appropriate department.'

Stanley's lips compressed tightly. He seemed about to defy Gently. Instead, he shrugged well-tailored shoulders and rose without another word.

The wage-accounts department of Metropolitan Electric was housed on the second floor of the new executive block. They went up to it in a lift which was heated and quite noiseless; it bore the company's trade-plate on its chaste ivory panelling. Stanley, still saying nothing, led them into the brightly lit offices, down an aisle between banks of desks and into a smaller, glass-partitioned room. Here, at desks of weathered sycamore, sat the head accountant and his lieutenants; the former a heavy-built, grey jowled man with sleeked black hair and a small moustache. At Stanley's approach he rose. He gave them a deferential smile.

'This is Dunmore, our wages chief, Superintendent. Dunmore, Superintendent Gently of the C.I.D.'

Dunmore seemed trying to decide whether this called for a handshake, but after a tentative movement with his hand he dropped it again nervously. Stanley congratulated him with a grunt. He said:

'The superintendent has a query. He appears to think we can tell him something about this Kincaid who used to work here. I feel certain we've nothing for him, but of course we must assist the police. So if you know anything about Kincaid, don't be afraid to come out with it.'

Dunmore looked worried. 'But wasn't he here rather a long time ago, sir?'

'He was, Dunmore. Twenty-two years ago, I'm told.'

Dunmore brightened. 'Then I'm afraid I couldn't know anything about him, sir. I was with Intrics, like yourself, sir. I didn't come here until the merger.'

'What about Wilson, Dunmore?'

'No, sir. He was with me at Intrics.'

'Spence? Baker?'

'We can ask them, sir. But I feel positive you'll find . . .'

He went through the farce of summoning his junior assistants, but one saw at a glance that they were strictly post-Kincaid. Baker, a man of forty, remembered hearing about him when he joined the firm, but even hearsay was dead by the time Spence had arrived there. Gently tried a pass at Baker.

'When did you join Met. L?'

'In nineteen–forty. I escaped war service on medical grounds.'

'Who told you about Kincaid?'

'Oh, it was just general talk. He was famous in a sort of way, and his having been here gave us a kick.'

45

'Name some people in this department who were here in nineteen-forty.'

'That isn't easy . . . there were a lot of changes made here during the war. People left and didn't come back; most of the clerical staff were temporaries. Bayntun, he knew Kincaid, but he went west at Tobruk . . .'

'Give me just one name.'

Baker glanced uneasily at Stanley. 'I don't think I can. The war changed things so much . . .'

'You see?' Stanley broke in smilingly. 'We're being reasonable, Superintendent. But we just seem to lack the information you require.'

Gently stared at him; then he turned his back and stumped over to the door. Through it came the clatter of typewriters and the rhythmic cadence of computers. There were fifty employees in the room at least, sitting at desks, moving about with papers; girls, youths, men of Baker's age: they seemed a positive conspiracy of youth. Then a flash of light caught Gently's eye, reflected from the far corner of the room. The head of someone wearing glasses projected above a glassed-in cubicle. A thin face, steel-rimmed glasses, meagre hair turning grey: the man suddenly caught his eye and the head was abruptly withdrawn. Gently turned to the group behind him.

'Inspector, there's something I left in the car . . .'

As Evans approached Gently muttered in his ear:

'Talk to the bloke in the cubicle there!'

He strode back to Stanley, who was watching him intently.

'You know, I could make myself awkward about

this. If I thought it was worthwhile I could put a squad of men in here. There'd be a stink, I can tell you. You'd make the headlines all right.'

'But, Superintendent, we're trying—'

'What do you keep in those files?'

'There's nothing, I feel certain—'

'How am I to know that? You started off by lying to me, and you've done your best to head me off. As far as I can see you've prepared for this visit very thoroughly . . .'

It was a row and an enjoyable row, because indulged in deliberately. With a dozen deft touches Gently brought his man to the boil. It was the more humiliating for Stanley because his employees stood about him, wholly fascinated by the sight of their managing director being bullied. Certainly, nobody had seen Evans disappear into the cubicle, nobody had a moment to spare to interrupt his proceedings . . .

'I've a good mind to make a complaint to your superiors, Superintendent!'

When he was angry, Stanley's lips trembled and he snatched his head as he spoke.

'Good Lord, to come in here, trying to play the little Hitler – do you realize, do you understand—'

'I understand that you want to hide something.'

'In heaven's name, hide what?'

'I'd like to know that too, of course.'

'You've got an obsession, Superintendent! This is persecution, nothing less . . .'

For ten minutes Gently kept it going with a malicious pleasure. Stanley had asked for something of this sort and Gently was delighted to oblige. Then he saw Evans leave the cubicle and make a rounded sign with his thumb and finger; it was time to call a halt, to round off the entertainment gracefully . . .

'In any case, I'm dissatisfied with the result of my inquiries. I shall expect those records found without further delay.'

'We shall find them, make no mistake. I'll not have this sort of thing twice.'

'And on another occasion I suggest you don't play clever with the police.'

He marched off; not failing to catch the gleam of relief in Stanley's face; into the lift, over the carpets and down the steps to the waiting Wolseley. Evans pushed open the door for him; the driver backed them out of the courtyard. Behind them, high in the murky gloom, Met. L's neon sign blazed sinisterly.

'Did I hear you having a spat, man?'

Gently's grin betrayed his satisfaction. 'A frank exchange of views, perhaps. Did it buy us anything from the man in the corner?'

'Oh yes. It bought us a lot.'

'Who was the fellow?'

'His name is Piper. He's the senior wages clerk and he's been with the firm since nineteen-thirty.'

'Ah. And he *did* remember Kincaid?'

'He worked beside him for nearly three years.'

Gently snuggled down into his seat, fetched up his pipe, and put a match to it. He compressed the ash with his thumb, puffing. 'Good, he said. 'Let me have it.'

'Well, this Piper believes in Kincaid. He says he's

certain that it's the same man. He says he was always a bit of a card and used to have ideas about religion.'

'That tallies with our Kincaid.'

'So I thought. And there's more to come. He knew the girl who Kincaid married. She used to work for Metropolitan Electric too.'

'She worked for them too!'

'So he says. She was a comptometer operator in those days. Paula Blackman, he got the name right, and she lived with her mother in a flat on the King's Road. And Piper was keen on her himself; which is why his memory is so good. But Kincaid was the one she fancied and Piper's stayed a bachelor ever since.'

'She must have been quite a girl.'

'I got a similar impression.'

'Did he give you a description?'

'You bet he did. I wrote it down.' Evans brought out his notebook and thumbed over the pages. 'Here it is, the best I could get from him after a great deal of questioning. She stood five feet seven and a half. She had a fine figure and some glamorous legs. She had a lot of fine hair, a broad forehead, a delicate nose, a pale, clear complexion and a wideish, thin-lipped mouth. Oh, and a cultivated voice.'

'What was her colouring, confound him?'

'Ah, now there's the big snag, and likewise the reason why Kincaid couldn't remember it. She used to dye and peroxide her hair. Piper never knew its real colour. He's seen it everything between black and a strawberry blonde. He thinks – only thinks, mind you

– that it ought to have been golden brown; but if you get a hot suspect, never mind about her hair, man.'

'And her eyes?' Gently grunted. 'Does she switch those too?'

'No man. They stay grey, as far as Piper remembers.'

'She wouldn't be using contact lenses, come in six different colours?'

'Well, I didn't think to ask. But I've got Piper's phone number.'

'And that's the lot?'

'No, not quite. Here's another small item. It seems that Fleece used to work for the same firm in those days.'

'Fleece . . . !'

Evans winked evilly. 'I thought you'd like to hear about that. I've been saving it up special – a sort of titbit, like.'

'So there is a connection there!' Gently sucked in long puffs. This had got to be relevant, however awkwardly it fitted in. Kincaid, his wife, and Arthur Fleece had all been contemporaries at Metropolitan Electric, and for reasons unknown the present boss there wanted to hide this. Why? Was he affected by it personally? Or had someone put pressure on him? And if the latter, who had the power to put pressure on Stanley . . . ?

'Was Fleece in wage accounts?'

'No, he was a very junior executive. Assistant manager or some such, in a production department.'

'When did he leave Met. L?'

'Straight after the Everest expedition. Apparently he

came into a bit of money; then he started up on his own.'

'And then he married?'

'I wouldn't know, man. Now you've heard everything Piper told me. But it gives me a curious sort of sensation, as strong as any of Kincaid's.'

'About Mrs Fleece?'

'You're guessing, man.'

'Where does she live?'

'Out Kingston way.'

Gently tapped their driver's shoulder. 'Cut across to Kingston,' he said.

They switched to the North Circular and proceeded southwards towards Kew, the rain pattering down now and beating hard on the windscreen. Quite childishly, Gently began humming the old Air Force song, and immediately Evans chimed in with a strong, practised baritone:

She'll be coming round the mountains—
She'll be coming round the mountains—
She'll be coming round the mountains when
    she comes . . .

It was perhaps less than dignified, but wasn't this *l'affaire* Kincaid? Their driver caught the spirit; he came in strongly with the chorus.

CHAPTER FOUR

T HE FLEECE RESIDENCE in point of fact was in the
parish of Thames Ditton; it stood opposite the
eyot below Hampton Court and enjoyed the luxury of
a river frontage. A short, serpentine, gravelled drive
connected the house to the public road, curving its way
through paling willows whose leaves were descending
in the steady rain. The house which appeared was
stockbroker's Tudor, but of the less offensive type. Its
windows were plain, its timbering restrained and its
gables chaste and probably functional. Before the porch
the drive formed a roundabout in the island on which
were planted chrysanthemums, and to the right,
through a long pergola, one saw the lawns running
down to the river.

There were no lights in any of the windows, though
it was now becoming dusk, but a green and cream
sports car stood parked beside the roundabout. Gently
rang, and rang again. They could hear the sound of the
bell clearly; for nearly a minute, nevertheless, nobody
came to answer the summons. Then the light was

switched on in the porch overhead, a bolt drawn behind the door and the door itself opened.

'Mrs Fleece?'

'Y-yes. Who is it, please?'

She was a woman whose appearance checked with several firm clicks. Her height was approximately five feet seven, she had a strong-framed, slightly voluptuous figure, her hair was black, but had the sheen of dye on it, and her eyes were of a greyish hazel. She would be forty more or less, and was carelessly dressed in a black button-down frock. Her make-up was heavy and smeared and she had dark crescents beneath her eyes. She dispensed a heavy scent of carnations.

'Superintendent Gently, C.I.D.'

'Oh, I see. It's about Arthur again . . . ?'

'There's a little routine which we have to clear up.'

'Yes, naturally. Though I thought the people at Surbiton . . .

She stood dithering, as though reluctant to ask them into the house; her eyes frowning vacantly at a spot behind Gently.

'The servants are out . . . it's rather difficult. I wasn't expecting any callers. Up till yesterday I had the children at home here, too . . .

'We won't waste much of your time, Mrs Fleece.'

'Oh, I know. You have to do these things.'

'We're sorry to trouble you at a time like this.'

'No, that doesn't matter. I'm getting used to it, anyway . . .'

At last she made up her mind and stood back from the doorway. They entered, and she led them down a panelled hall and switched on the lights in a room at the end of it.

'If you'll wait in here, please, I'll be with you in a minute. I was just seeing to something. It's the servants' day out . . .'

Evans closed the door softly behind her and then turned to Gently with a grimace. 'Twenty-two years make a lot of difference, but that's life for you. It could well be her.'

Gently nodded. 'She'd have lost that complexion.'

'Aye. And she's dyeing her hair for a reason. But you can't get away from her eyes, nor the figure neither. She's still a fine woman.'

'I wonder . . .'

Gently wandered musingly round the large, pleasant room. It was a lounge, and had big bow windows which faced down the lawns to the river. The furniture was light and modern and over in a corner stood a miniature grand. A long, low couch in two-tone leather was placed back to the window; its cushions were crumpled. Evans was sniffing.

'Can you smell it too, man?'

Gently nodded again. 'Yes. Gold Block, isn't it?'

'Gold Block – that's it. I couldn't quite put a name to it.'

'And it's strictly a pipe tobacco.'

'Goodness gracious! She isn't a pipe-smoker?'

Gently smiled at him thinly. 'We'll perhaps hear the sequel in a minute.'

He had hardly spoken when they heard the sports car being started; a couple of full-throated roars, then a scrape of gears and the rattle of gravel. Evans started for the door, but Gently dropped a hand on his arm:

'Take it easy! You're too late, and it may not be our business anyway.'

'But she had a bloke in here!'

'That's not one hundred per cent criminal.'

'You don't know – it might be that Stanley. It might tie in good and proper.'

Gently shrugged, shaking his head. 'He couldn't have got over here ahead of us. Better be a sportsman, laddie. After all, it's the servants' day out . . .'

Evans relaxed, but he still looked indignant. 'The deadly wickedness of the world!' he said. 'And her old man still lying in the mortuary – due for burial Friday, they tell me.'

'There couldn't have been much love lost there.'

'You're telling me there couldn't, man.'

'It's a point that's worth remembering . . . and perhaps our driver can describe the bloke.'

When Mrs Fleece rejoined them she was looking inconspicuously neater and she darted a timid glance at them, as though anticipating comment. She chose a straight-backed chair and sat awkwardly, folding her hands in her lap. She said quickly:

'I had to let out the plumber. We've been having trouble with the drains . . .'

Evans raised his eyes to the ceiling, where the prospect seemed to fascinate him.

Gently said: 'We'd like some information about your husband, Mrs Fleece. It's a painful subject, I'm afraid, but we'll be as brief as we can. When were you married to him, by the way?'

'When? Oh, in nineteen-thirty-nine.' She appeared surprised by the question, but she answered it quite readily.

'Had you known him for very long?'

'Well, a year or two, I think.'

'How did you come to be acquainted?'

'I met him at a party my mother gave. Actually' – she gave her shoulders a twist – 'he was brought there by a friend of mine. I probably behaved very badly – Sally was awfully cut up, poor girl. But I really couldn't help it, and it's such a long time ago . . .

'And when was that?'

'Oh, years ago. Before he went on the expedition. They were planning it at the time, so it would be the autumn of nineteen-thirty-six. I remember Arthur taking me somewhere to look at their equipment – odd sort of tents and weird gas-masks, and the most frightful-looking food. It was all very expensive and I could never see the point of it.'

'Did you meet other members of the expedition?'

'I – well, I met some of them.'

'Which ones, Mrs Fleece?'

'Er, well . . . there was Dick Overton.'

'Who else?'

'I don't know . . . there were several. I don't remember.'

'But you do remember Reginald Kincaid?'

'No. I never actually met him.'

Her reactions were curious; Gently couldn't quite fathom them. For instance, his question about Kincaid had the effect of relieving a mounting distress. As though it were somehow a safer subject, she added hurriedly:

'But I knew about him, of course. He used to work for the same people as Arthur, and Arthur told me of his funny ways.'

'Didn't you ever see him at the works?'

'Me? How should I? I never went there. It was before Arthur started on his own, an electrical firm in North London somewhere. I was doing secretarial work for a business agency in Balham – Dyson's, that was the place. They've moved to Lambeth now, I believe.'

'What was your maiden name, Mrs Fleece?'

'Amies. Sarah Amies.'

'And you've always lived in Fulham?'

'Fulham? Never – did I say I'd lived in Fulham?'

'I understood that your mother lived there.'

'Oh no; you've been misinformed. Actually, I was born not far from Dorking. Then we took the house in Kensington when' – she shrugged – 'when Mother's divorce came through.'

'And your mother still lives in Kensington?'

'No. She died ten years ago.'

All this was quite cool and without a sign of hesitation. Now she opened her handbag and lit a cigarette. It was baffling. Her fingers were trembling and she was obviously ill at ease, yet by all the signs this had nothing to do with either Kincaid or her identity. If she was Paula Kincaid, was she so certain of her ground? And if so, what was the subject which was making that little lighter tremble?

'Where were you and Mr Fleece married?'

She snatched eagerly at the question. 'At Penwood near Dorking, where my home used to be. My mother had some friends there and I was married from their place – it's a pretty little church, it's got an avenue of yew trees.'

'A white wedding . . .'

'Oh, yes. Orange blossom and white lilac. It was at Whitsun, you see, just after the crisis. We'd been going to the Black Forest . . . it's such a long time ago.'

'What was the name of your mother's friends?'

'Wait . . . I'll remember it in a minute. They were elderly people of about Mother's age. They lived in a house not far from the church. Baxter or Blackstable . . . I'm sorry, I'm not certain. Arthur was the one who remembered names . . .'

'Was your marriage a happy one?'

She faltered at that. For a second or two Gently thought she intended to challenge the question. But she didn't, she rallied.

'Oh yes . . . I think you'd say so. But latterly, of course, Arthur's been terribly busy.'

'With business you mean?'

'Yes, business took up his time. I don't think he always realized how much I was alone.'

'Was he away from home often?'

'Yes; and the children, they're at school. We've twins, you know. A son and a daughter.'

'But naturally you'd have friends?'

'Well, that's not quite the same.'

'People like – Mr Stanley, for example?'

58

'Him?' She shook her head definitely. 'We're not in his class; he's a millionaire or something. Arthur knew him through the business, but I've only met him once or twice.'

'What about Dick Overton?'

He saw the cigarette shudder.

'I haven't met him for years. None of the Everest Club members.'

'Didn't you go to their annual dinners?'

'No – no, they were just for members . . .'

'Weren't you on the ramble last week?'

'Good God, no! I was here . . . in London . . .

'In this house?'

'No, not in this house. At a hotel. I wanted a change.'

'Which hotel, Mrs Fleece?'

'The Suffolk in Knightsbridge. Does it really matter?'

It did; that was clear from the way she was taking it. Her free hand was on her breast; she had leant forward; her cheeks were pale. She suddenly burst out:

'What does all this matter, anyway? Kincaid killed him; you know he did. Can't you leave the rest alone . . . ?'

Gently hunched his shoulders wearily and stared at the darkened panes of the window: Stanley had said the same thing in his more calculated way. Kincaid wasn't to be probed, he was to remain an enigma; they could hang him or lock him up if they liked, but they mustn't unreasonably seek the truth . . .

He said: 'You were acquainted with your husband for nearly three years before you married him?'

She nodded and he sensed again that he was wide of that which worried her.

'That's a long time surely?'

'He wanted to get on his feet. He left his job after the expedition and set up his own firm.'

'He had capital, did he?'

'Yes. He came into some money.'

'It was left him?'

'He didn't tell me . . . no, I don't think it was that.'

'Why don't you think it was that?'

'Oh, just the way he spoke about it. He was awfully pleased with himself, as though he'd done something clever.'

'Was it a loan from someone?'

'No, I'm sure it wasn't.'

'From one of the club members?'

Crash! – he was back in the target area.

'He had nothing to do with the club members. He only met them twice a year!' Her eyes flamed. She strained towards him like a bitch protecting its litter. 'It was just a tradition, that precious club, it didn't mean anything to anybody. They'd drifted apart. They were strangers. The club bored Arthur stiff!'

'So you didn't meet any of them again?'

Mrs Fleece groaned. 'I told you so.'

'Not even Dick Overton, with whom you were acquainted?'

'I simply mentioned his name. It was the only one I could think of.'

Gently hesitated. He wondered whether to press the matter further. There was oil in it somewhere, of that

60

he was certain. But whether it touched on what they had come after was another matter again: he was groping in the dark for facts which were largely undefined. He rose to his feet slowly.

'There may be other questions, Mrs Fleece.'

'I suppose so.'

She rose also, smoothing her black widow's dress.

'In the meantime I'd like to borrow a good photograph of your husband . . . one with you on it too, if you've got one to spare.'

'You're perfectly welcome.'

Without demur she went to a small ebony cabinet and fetched from it an album, which she handed to Gently. It was filled with postcard-size and larger prints showing the usual domestic subjects: mostly herself and the two children, against a variety of backgrounds. In the few which included her husband the photos were less skilfully taken but there was one, a regular portrait, of a much greater merit.

'A friend of ours did that. He's exceptionally good with a camera.'

Gently removed it from its mount and spent a moment or two studying it. It showed Fleece full-face, wearing a lumberjack shirt, a piton in his hand, and a slight smile on his lips. His pendulous nose gave a Semitic cast to his pale, oval face; the skull, egg-shaped, made a polished cone above a scanty fringe of hair. His eyes and ears were both small, his neck short, his shoulders bowed. The eyes were light-coloured and looked disparaging. They were almost sneering at the photographer.

'Is this a recent photograph of your husband?'

Why did spots of colour appear in her cheeks?

'Yes, quite recent. This summer. It's the last one I have of him.'

'Who took it?'

'Just . . . just a friend. He wouldn't like his name brought into it.'

Gently grunted and searched on through the album for a revealing shot of Sarah Fleece. He found one loose in the back, unmistakably a counterpart to that of her husband. It was taken against the same background and showed a similar technical skill, but in this instance the smile of the sitter was unalloyed by any sneer. Sarah Fleece looked radiantly beautiful, her dark hair loosened, her grey eyes sparkling.

'Your friend is certainly an excellent photographer.'

'Yes . . . of course, that's another of his.'

'I'll borrow these two if I may.'

'Yes, certainly.' But she seemed reluctant. 'I'll get them back again, won't I?'

'They'll be returned in a few days.'

He gravely wrote out the receipt while she was finding him an envelope, then she accompanied them to the door, the receipt still held in her hand. On the steps Gently turned.

'You'll be called at the trial, naturally. But would you have any objection to seeing Kincaid in his cell?'

She gave a gasp. 'No – no! Not that!'

'You have specific reasons for refusing?'

'I couldn't. I couldn't. Not the man who did that to Arthur!'

Gently touched the brim of his trilby. 'We wouldn't press you, of course, Mrs Fleece . . .'

Back in the Wolseley Evans tackled their driver about the owner of the sports car, but the circumstances had been against any accurate observation. The man had appeared from the rear of the house and had entered his car on its far side, while their driver had had no reason to be especially curious about him.

'It was raining like the devil and he'd got his collar turned up; a bloke around five feet ten, light-coloured raincoat and peakless cap. He was medium build and looked light on his feet. His age I wouldn't like to say. The car was a new Austin-Healey.'

Gently looked at Evans. 'Does that suggest anyone to you?'

Evans shook his head regretfully. 'Not a soul, man,' he said. 'I was hoping he would tie up with one of the Everest Club people, because she seemed a little tender when you got on to them.'

'Could it have been Richard Overton?'

'It could and it couldn't. He's about that height and of a medium sort of build. It would help to know about his car.'

'We'll check all their cars while we're at it. We may be throwing away our time, but you can never know too much.'

He directed their driver to Bow Street and then switched on the car's radio. By the exchange he was connected to the homicide charge-room. He asked for Dutt and was lucky: the Tottenham sergeant had just come in; within moments he had taken over the line at the other end.

'This is the Kincaid business, Dutt. I want you to run an errand for me. Go over to the Suffolk Hotel in Knightsbridge and check there on a Mrs Arthur Fleece. She's supposed to have spent the weekend there and I'd like all the detail you can get: what nights, whether visited, and if absent for any considerable period. Her Christian name is Sarah. Over.'

Dutt's cheerful voice came back to him. 'Yessir. Mrs Arthur or Sarah Fleece. Where would you like to have the report, sir?'

'I'll be in my office in about an hour.'

Next he got on to Information and asked them to contact Dorking. He gave them a résumé of Mrs Fleece's information about her wedding.

'The church register isn't enough. I want the details investigated. Especially the Baxter-Blackstable people, and the names of anybody who knew the Amies.'

He switched off, lit his pipe and remained silent for some moments, watching the wet Putney streets as the Wolseley hissed through them; then, as the Thames swept darkly under them, he blew an inquisitive ring at Evans.

'Come on. Let's be having it. You've got a dozen theories by now . . .'

Evans grinned at him, nodding. 'You knew, I can't keep my mind still. It's a disease with us Welshmen; we've got unsettled brains. But I was just setting it up in a proper order so to speak; trying to fit it all in and to make out a pattern.'

Gently puffed. 'It begins at Met. L.'

'Aye. The three of them there together. Fleece, Kincaid, and Paula Blackman; three small people out of thousands. Now, Fleece and Kincaid probably know each other because they're both keen on climbing, and they have to be known by some of these other people or they wouldn't have been chosen for the expedition. By the way, we don't know much about that, how it was organized and financed.'

'We'll talk to Overton tomorrow. He should be able to throw some light on it.'

'A good idea, man. But to continue. We will take a hypothesis. Fleece is smitten by Paula Kincaid, and Paula Kincaid is not indifferent to him. In the light of that, view the expedition, of which remember Fleece was the leader, and the opportunity it gave him of quietly doing away with Kincaid. There wasn't any violence called for: Fleece might have drawn a line at violence. But it was as good a way as another and in my book it stands as murder.'

'Provided,' Gently inserted, 'Kincaid's story is the true one.'

'Provided that of course. I must admit to prejudice there. Well, Fleece comes back to England to console the widow, and it may or may not be relevant that he came into money just then. But he sets up in business and he marries Mrs Kincaid, and it goes like a song for twenty-two years. Then this fellow turns up, this so-called Kincaid. He has a nasty story to tell and he's determined to find his wife. What would you expect Fleece to do about it? Why, exactly what he did do.

He would try to discredit the man, he'd go to law to stop his mouth. But either Kincaid had a friend or Fleece had an enemy, because someone told Kincaid where to look for his wife. Then it was Everest all over again with, this time, Kincaid as the survivor. Man, it's justice when you look at it. It's almost a shame for us to step in.'

Gently said unkindly: 'You've forgotten the cigarette-case.'

'Oh, but I haven't.' Evans faced him in triumph. 'You worried me about that, so I took special note of it. And I can tell you who dropped it. It was Fleece himself.'

Gently nodded twice, reluctantly. 'Yes, man. That's *brilliant*.'

'Isn't it obvious when you think of it? Who else was so likely to have had the case?'

'It's obviousness is a little contingent. It depends on the identity of Mrs Fleece.'

'But either way, man, it's the answer. It answers the objection about the case.'

Evans sat nursing his triumph as they passed through Chelsea, where the teatime traffic began to build up around them. Then he said:

'I wouldn't bank too much on any theory about Kincaid, but I'm telling you now that I have a certain small confidence. He's going to recognize that photograph; then we'll confront her with him. And the rest can go hang. We'll have our case sewn up.'

'Wouldn't you like to know the identity of Mrs Fleece's latest?'

Evans chuckled. 'I would, too. I'm afraid he's a dirty dog, that one.'

At Bow Street, which was smelling even sootier and damper, Kincaid was fetched from his cell and given a chair. He looked unhappy, but he brightened when his eye fell on Gently; then his expression changed again, to one of pettish irritation. He said:

'I've been talking to my lawyer, and he won't do what I tell him.'

Gently shrugged. 'They won't always. What did you want him to do?'

'I told you that. I asked him to search for evidence to establish my identity, but he refused point-blank to do it until after my trial was over. I shall change him, of course. I don't put up with that sort of thing.'

Evans murmured: 'You may find lawyers a little difficult, man.'

Gently produced the critical photograph, but he held it with its back towards Kincaid. The latter immediately fixed his eyes on it, regarding it with a tremulous sort of fascination. Gently waited. Kincaid's emotion grew with each added moment; till finally, unable to bear it longer, he gave a little sob and reached out his hand.

'Is that my w-wife you've got there?'

'How would you recognize her, Kincaid?'

'I'd know – I would. Oh please let me see her!'

'She had grey eyes, hadn't she?'

Kincaid's own eyes opened wider.

'She used to dye her hair, didn't she? Her complexion was pale and clear?'

Kincaid's hand flew to his mouth. His breath came

in a ragged gasp. He stared idiot-like at Gently, his teeth were cutting into his fingers.

'Isn't that how you'd know her?'

Kincaid gave a strangled cry. 'Yes . . . yes!' He went on repeating it in a hysterical gabble.

Gently reversed the photograph and thrust it into Kincaid's hand. The man seized it, bent over it, twisting himself away from Gently. Then the tension seemed to snap in him and he began to laugh uncontrollably. He dropped the photograph on the floor, a smear of blood on it from his hand.

'Is *that* your wife, Kincaid?'

He only laughed the more. Though they waited for half an hour, they could get nothing sensible out of him.

CHAPTER FIVE

Alas for Evans's confidence! It was to have very little to bolster it, and by the time they called it a day all his original gloom had returned. No sudden solution was round the corner, no neat tying of the ends, rather the indications were that they were getting further away from the mark.

Dutt was waiting in Gently's office when they returned to the Yard. They found him immersed in an evening paper in which Kincaid still rated the headlines. Gently took it from him. The headlines ran:

FRESH MOVES IN KINCAID SAGA
Supt. Gently Visits Bow Street
Surprise Enquiries at Hendon

'That's one in the eye for our friend, Mr Stanley.'

Evans snorted. He was reading the item over Gently's shoulder. He was much intrigued by the accompanying picture, which showed himself and Gently alighting from the Wolseley. Gently gave him the paper and sat down. He'd seen too many of these things.

'Was the lady on record?' he asked Dutt.

'Yessir.' Dutt drew out his notebook. 'But she wasn't under the name you gave me, though.'

'Wasn't she then? So how did you get on to her?'

'What you might call coincidence, sir. One of the maids there used to work for her, and I chanced to catch her at the desk.'

'Good for you.'

Gently nodded congratulations and Dutt looked pleased. Evans tore himself away from the picture to stare interrogatively at the sergeant. Dutt continued:

'She gives the name of Mrs Sterling, sir, but the maid knew well enough that she was Arthur Fleece's missus. Said she lived at Thames Ditton and was wife of the bloke what was murdered – about forty, a smart sort of woman, wears her hair dyed black.'

Evans groaned. 'That's her, man.'

Dutt turned over a page. 'She booked in at the Suffolk on 16th September and left again last Monday. She was in a bit of a hurry.'

'September 16th?'

'Yessir. That's correct.'

Gently met Evans's eye. 'So she was there for three weeks . . . Was she absent during that time?'

'No sir. She never went out much. Just shopping and such-like, and once or twice to a show. She used to write a lot of letters and she used the phone quite a bit, but it was always the paybox in the hall, so I couldn't trace the calls.'

'What about visitors?'

'Yessir, I made a note of them. She had her kids there the first weekend; twins they are, about eleven or twelve. Then there was an elderly, professional bloke who called to see her a couple of times – a grey-haired geezer, on the tall side, wore a black suit and carried a briefcase. That's the lot, apart from a bloke who drove her home once or twice. But he never got out of his car so I couldn't get his particulars.'

'Did you get a description of the car?'

'Yessir. A sports job.'

'A green and cream Austin-Healey?'

'The porter didn't notice, sir.'

'That's a pity. What happened on Monday?'

'She got a trunk call, sir, from Llanberis. It came in around half-past five when she was having tea in the lounge. She took the call at the hall desk and the clerk moved off so's not to look nosey, but from the way she behaved he's pretty certain what it was about. She turned as pale as a ghost and ordered a double brandy. Then she went up and packed, and she was off by half-past six.'

'Any other details?'

'She had a letter on most days, sir. The address was typewritten, to Mrs Sterling, and they were posted in the London area.'

'Thanks, Dutt. You've done a nice job.'

'Just a bit of routine, sir.'

'Tell them to send us up a snack, will you? We're going to wait here for a call.'

Dutt departed, leaving his paper as a souvenir for

Evans. But the big Welshman was no longer enthralled by his front-page billing. He said mournfully:

'It either means something or else it does not – and either way I can't see it helping Myfanw Evans.'

'How do you read it?' Gently asked.

Evans laid a finger to his nose. 'A divorce, man, large as life. Fleece was preparing to give her the push.'

'But if she happened to be Paula Kincaid?'

'Stop rubbing it in. I can see a barn door. If she happened to be Paula Kincaid then the marriage was probably void in any case.'

Gently shook his head. 'I'm not so sure. It's a legal point worth settling. But his reason for divorcing her seems plain enough. She has a boyfriend in the offing.'

'And he could be an Everest Club member.'

'That's almost certain on the facts. The call from Llanberis didn't come from the police – unless your Welsh police happen to be psychic. They had no reason to contact a Mrs Sterling staying at the Suffolk Hotel in Knightsbridge.'

'Glory be, that never struck me! Of course, it has to be one of the members.'

'And if you're thinking the way I'm thinking . . .'

Evans looked sick. 'Raymond Heslington,' he said.

'He was the one with the opportunity. He may not be the one with the car.'

Gently opened a drawer of his desk and fetched out the file on Kincaid. Inside it, prominent amongst the statements, was that of Heslington, containing his particulars. Gently rang Information:

'Note this name and address. I want a description of his car; just the make and colouring will do.'

While they waited Evans's face seemed to grow sadder and sadder and not even the advent of coffee and sandwiches served to relieve his dolour. He munched largely but unfeelingly, a steady mechanical champ, and took big mouthfuls of coffee without looking at his cup. He was either up or down. There were no half-measures with Evans.

'I can see it all now. I'm the biggest arse going. He lied to me, that fellow, and I swallowed it down to the tail. Never thought, never doubted; just trusted my own stupid judgement. I could see a wonderful case, man, and I couldn't see anything else.'

'He might still have been telling the truth,' Gently mumbled over a sandwich.

'No he mightn't, man. I can sense it. We can forget about Kincaid. He was just a red herring, he happened along very convenient.'

'Heslington's description fitted him, didn't it?'

'What sort of a description was that? A brown jacket and grey slacks – and he might have seen him somewhere, anyway. No, no, you'll never convince me now that Kincaid was up there. I have an instinct, I tell you. My promotion is down the drain.'

At that moment the phone went. Gently limbered it to his ear. Evans watched his face fearfully, trying to read there his own perdition. Better men than Evans, however, had failed to read Gently's poker face, and the call turned out to be a longer one than the description of a car would require. Gently reached for a pad and pencil and scribbled down some unintelligible notes. Finally, he adjured his telespondent to try again in the morning. He hung up and sighed humorously.

'It's been and done it on us again.'

'Who was that, man?' Evans asked.

'Dorking, reporting on Sarah Amies. They've never heard of her in Penwood. They've never heard of Baxter or Blackstable. The village church has been converted to a hall and they can't for the moment lay hands on the register. Penwood is one of the new overspill areas. Most of the original inhabitants have hopped it.'

Evans gestured with shoulders and hand. 'Does it matter now, the way things are?'

'It matters to me, if nobody else. I've been told off to identify Kincaid.'

'But if Heslington is Mrs Fleece's boyfriend—'

The phone buzzed again to interrupt him. This time, while Gently listened, an expression did flit over his face. He replaced the phone. He dusted his hands.

'All right,' he said. 'That's that for the evening. Heslington's car is a new Ford Anglia. It's Cambridge blue, and its been garaged all day.'

Evans was staying in a wretched hotel in the vicinity of Euston Station, and Gently, still feeling responsible for him, invited him home to his Finchley rooms. Elphinstone Road was a gem of its kind. It had come into being during the eighteen sixties; a sedate thoroughfare, little disturbed by traffic, with public gardens on one side and ice-cake villas on the other. Its atmosphere had always held a charm for Gently. It was hansom cab, parasol, hard hat, and bustle skirt. The teardrop street lamps had never been ravished and war had spared the cast-iron railings, while of twenty complacent villas, twenty still lined Elphinstone Road.

Evans, who came in glum and silent, soon warmed to the snugness of Gently's retreat. He browsed over the books and the photographs and the fishing rods, and the big stuffed pike with its glassy eye. He too was an angler, it appeared, though his talk was of Gwyniads and bottomless llyns; and by the time they'd eaten supper and were sitting over the fire his mercurial spirits were once more to rights.

'But I don't mind telling you I'm foxed by all this. We've had plenty of bites, but we never strike a fish.'

'All the same, it's interesting. Some of the bites are unexpected. We were using paste over at Hendon, but we got a pike-size in nibbles.'

'He's a deadly liar, man, is that Mr Stanley.'

Gently yawned. 'I agree ... he's also an actor of some talent. And still the questions are: what's behind it? Why was he covering up on Kincaid? Why didn't he want us to meet Piper and get the information we did from him?'

'Do you think it's her he was protecting?'

'That's a very seductive theory. Fleece was in the same line of business; there'd be an *esprit de l'électricité* or something. They're both liars, Stanley and her. We can't take their words for the extent of the acquaintance. And if Mrs Fleece is Paula Kincaid, she'd have reason enough to want it kept quiet.'

'But where does the bloke in the sports car come into it?'

'Where indeed? We shall have to know that. And there's another idea that's struck me. We may have jumped at the divorce angle too quickly.'

'How do you mean, man?'

'Can't you see the alternative? Kincaid was moving heaven and earth to find her. She may have been using the hotel as a hideout when his inquiries were getting too close.'

'Aye. That's possible too.'

'And one of the club members may have been in the secret. That would account for her getting that trunk-call. The sports car johnny may be a blind.'

A grin spread delightedly over Evans' face. 'Man,' he said, 'you're cheering me up something wonderful. But what about Kincaid's reaction to that picture — you aren't going to tell me you accept it as positive?'

'He talked to his lawyer, don't forget.'

'I know. And little good it seems to have done him.'

'I wouldn't be so sure of that. Kincaid is far from being a simpleton. He may have decided to change his mind about his policy of being himself; in which case he wouldn't recognize fifty photographs of his wife. And we'd be the more likely to believe him if he kept up the pretence, so why should he drop it? His course of action is plain.'

'That's a beautiful piece of reasoning, and I wish I could believe it.'

Gently chuckled. He tapped out his pipe on the serpentine bar of the grate. 'Tomorrow we'll do some more fishing. We'll cast a line in Fleece's business. And perhaps a little quiet ledgering in the Everest Club waters.'

The morning was fugitively fine with a bright sun among darkling clouds. In the gardens across the way the autumn trees steamed and sparkled. Gently was finding it rather pleasant to have a guest sharing his breakfast routine, even though the papers were subdivided and his reading time was diminished. Evans was enjoying himself too and his appetite delighted Mrs Jarvis. Her cousin had married a Welshman, she told them, and really he was quite like one of the family . . .

The arrival of their Wolseley put an end to the domestic interlude. Fleece's firm, Electroproducts, had an address at Ilford. They took the North Circular Road, bending through Edmonton and Woodford, the great reaching arc that spanned the metropolis like a dome. Electroproducts occupied a site not far from Seven Kings station. One saw at a glance that it was unable to challenge comparison with its vast competitor at Hendon. A range of plain crook-roofed buildings, some subsidiary sheds and erections and a yard enclosed with wire mesh: these comprised its entirety. In the yard was a roofed rack in which cycles were stacked. Beside it were parked a few cars and a number of scooters and motorcycles. The office section, a long lean-to at the side of the workshops, was approached through fence-gates which stood open and unattended.

They drove in and parked. They were met by no palatial reception. Beyond the door was a narrow passage which received a dim light from the work-shops. A girl came hurrying out of a doorway with a sheaf of work sheets in her hand. She stopped on seeing the two detectives and stared inquiringly before asking:

'You want Mr Bemmells, is it?'

Mr Bemmells was the general manager; he was a lean and hard-faced man of about fifty-five or so. He had a haggard, harassed look, his eyebrows slanting down from the centre, but this seemed a natural condition with him and no reflection of the current circumstances. He found them seats in his cluttered office and listened attentively to Gently's preface.

'So you want to know how we started up? Then you've come to the right person. I was in this firm from the beginning, back in nineteen-thirty-eight. We were in Walthamstow then, in a converted warehouse in Sibley Street, and we stayed there till forty-two, when Jerry copped us with incendiaries. Then we moved to this site – a priority job, building this was; we were turning out aircraft stuff in those days, cable conduit, jennies, starters. Then after the war we went back to appliances – you've probably seen our products about – and now we're working up an export connection besides our regular contract work. That's the story of Electroproducts: a good investment, if I may say so.'

Gently grinned. 'I'll have to mention the name to my stockbroker. But I'd like more detailed information about the way the firm was formed. How did you come to be associated with it?'

'I answered an advert in our trade journal. I was with London Insulated at the time and finding promotion rather slow. So I took a chance with a new firm, and I've never regretted it. We've been expanding all the time and we've acquired a site for a new premises.'

'Was the firm organized when you joined it?'

'No. It was just in the process. But Mr Fleece had formed a nucleus of technical staff and designers.'

'Were there share issues at that stage?'

'No, that came a little later.'

'Where did the initial capital come from?'

Bemmells looked blank. 'From Mr Fleece, I suppose.'

'Did he mention how it was acquired?'

'Not to me he didn't. But then it wasn't my business. There's no question about it, is there?'

'Nothing of any importance.' Gently's tone was reassuring. 'But since you're second-in-command here I thought that Fleece might have dropped you a hint. You were fairly intimate with him, were you?'

'Our relations were always excellent.'

'You met his wife and family of course?'

'I did on occasion. I've been invited to his home.'

'Did you go to his wedding in thirty-nine?'

'No . . . it occurred out of town, I believe.'

'Did you know his wife before he married her?'

'I'm afraid I didn't. I moved in rather different circles.'

Gently made a break. Bemmells' expression had become increasingly wary, as though by degrees it was dawning on him that all was not entirely innocent. He flickered looks from Gently to the desk and again to Evans; but he didn't, as Gently hoped, come out with something unsolicited.

'Mrs Fleece told us that her husband was often away from home on business. That's something you'd know about. Where did his business use to take him?'

'Wherever there was a chance of a contract. Mr Fleece was all business. He's been as far as Pakistan – South Africa – the West Indies.'

'Had he been abroad lately?'

'He went to Holland in the spring. And just lately he'd made one or two trips into Wales.'

'Into Wales? What was that for?'

'He didn't tell me, I'm afraid. He simply mentioned that he had business there which needed following up.'

'Could you give a shrewd guess?'

Bemmells frowned. 'There's the Conway project. Or the installation at Corwen. We might contract for either of those.'

'Wouldn't he have told you about that? Wouldn't he have taken a technical adviser with him?'

'It would have been more usual, I admit. But it was entirely up to him.'

Gently could hear Evans's feet stirring: this was interesting information! A coincidence it might be, but it had a tendentious ring to it. Had Fleece's trips been on business his manager would surely have been in his confidence, and had they been personal . . . what personal reason would have taken Fleece to Wales?

'Exactly when did these trips take place?'

'I didn't make a note of them, naturally. But the first one was in August during the week following our works' fortnight. There were two or three in

80

September and another last week: four or five altogether. Then, of course, there was last weekend.'

'On what days of last week?'

Bemmells considered. 'The Tuesday and Wednesday.'

'Was that the usual length of the visits?'

'Oh yes. A couple of days.'

'Would he have driven down by car?'

'Yes. He rarely used the trains.'

'At what address were you supposed to contact him?'

'I never did, because he didn't leave one.'

'And your works' fortnight – when was that?'

'At the usual time. The first two weeks in August.'

In effect, Fleece's trips had begun a few days after Kincaid's appearance: and had continued at frequent intervals until a fatal one supervened.

'Have you anything to add to this, Mr Bemmells? It could have some bearing on Fleece's death.'

'No . . . I assure you. That's all I know about it.' Bemmells had paled as this aspect was put to him.

'There's one other matter, touching Mr Fleece's personal life. It's important, you understand, or I wouldn't be asking about it. Would you say he was happily married?'

A mottled flush replaced Bemmells' pallor. 'I – I'm not quite certain if I should answer that question. There was a coolness between them, I believe, from certain things Mr Fleece said . . . and I did have the impression . . . but it's nothing I want to repeat.'

'I'm not idly curious, Mr Bemmells. Was your impression that she had a lover?'

'I . . . well!' Bemmells was rocked. He looked

81

heartily uncomfortable. 'Yes, I certainly had the impression of – er – something of that sort. Mr Fleece said cynical things . . . not always seriously, I may add.'

'Did he cynically mention a name?'

'No. No name was mentioned. Believe me, I never knew anything for a fact.'

'Was a divorce talked about?'

'Well . . . very loosely, he did refer to it . . .'

'In that case I'd like the name and address of his solicitors.'

Bemmells found it for him, quite flustered, spilling papers over his desk. The solicitors were Agnew, Sharp, and Adams and the address in the Temple. Bemmells followed them out to the car, fluttering around them like a broody hen, and at last he screwed up his courage to ask:

'It won't affect the poor lady's rights, will it . . . ?'

When they drove away towards the city Evans was doubled up with laughter. He appeared to have found something unbearably comic about the manager of Electroproducts.

'Suppose – just suppose for the moment – suppose he's the co-respondent himself, man!'

The idea was too much for him. He almost sobbed with mirth.

Gently wasn't so much amused and he filled and lit his pipe sombrely. Something had clicked in his mind when he'd heard of those visits to Wales. It was as though then, for the first time, he'd made a genuine connection with the case; as though at that moment, from all the heaped uncertainty, something certain had fallen into his hand. There was no logical reason for this. There never was in these matters. At the best it was a dark motion in a carefully prepared unconscious. But he knew the signal when it reached him and it had reached him now: he was positive that those visits were part of the pattern he was seeking. Evans too, when he'd controlled his chortling, found something disturbing in the information.

'Are you thinking, man, that Fleece stirred up something in Wales?'

Gently hunched. 'I haven't got round to being definitive,' he replied.

'That was a peculiar little timetable which the Bemmells lad gave us. I had a sensation we were on to something which didn't overplease me.'

'It has to do with Kincaid somehow, if it affects the case at all. Kincaid's appearance triggered those visits. They follow each other much too neatly.'

'Goodness gracious, you give me ideas. Couldn't Kincaid also have made trips to Wales? Couldn't that be the reason for Fleece's going there, to keep an eye on the foolish fellow?'

'In what connection?' Gently exhaled smoke.

'Why, I don't know. But I'll do some imagining. Suppose Mrs Fleece isn't Paula Kincaid, and suppose they both went to Wales in search of her? Kincaid, he's got a notion she'll be there, and Fleece, he's got a notion that Kincaid's got a notion. So he follows Kincaid about in the hope that he'll lead him to Mrs Kincaid, and in the end Kincaid gets tired of it and gives Fleece a shove over Snowdon.'

Gently chuckled among his smoke-wreaths. 'And why should Fleece want to meet her so badly?'

'Well, man, I reckon I've done my bit – you'll have to imagine the rest for yourself!'

They both laughed, but then they grew thoughtful again: Evans's fancy wasn't as bizarre as he had made it sound. Fleece's visits to Wales had begun and ended with Kincaid; was it stretching matters much to suppose a correspondence in between?

'Anyway, we netted one small tiddler,' Gently mused. 'We've confirmed the divorce angle, and soon we'll know who the beau is.'

Evans nodded. 'Though I'm looking on the bright side,' he said. 'He could be someone quite harmless, notwithstanding that trunk-call.'

They came in down the Mile End Road, through Whitechapel and past the Bank, with Evans craning his neck to view the sooty antiquity of St Paul's; and then off Fleet Street into the quieter waters of the Temple, where the sun, still holding its own, brightened the quadrangles and sad trees. Agnew, Sharp, and Adams had chambers overlooking the Garden. There Gently's inquiry, after a legal interval, gained them the audience of the second partner.

'Yes, I handled Fleece's affairs. Also those of Electroproducts.' Mr Sharp belied his name; he resembled an affable country squire. 'I'd like to put in a claim for privilege but it would scarcely wash, would it? Death is the great *nolle prosequi*, and takes advice from no lawyer. What do you gentlemen want to know?'

'We've got four questions,' Gently replied.

'Four only? Then you're more economical than most policemen of my acquaintance. What's number one?'

'Can you tell us where Fleece got the capital to start in business?'

'Not I, sir. But he had some. He was never short of cash.'

'Number two. Had he started a divorce suit?'

'Answer. Yes, he had.'

'Number three. When did he start it?'

'Answer. Let me get his file.'

From a row of venerable and dusty box files Sharp pulled out one with a new label: the last of a considerable sequence which had been pasted on it during past decades. He opened it and took out some papers.

'Fleece first consulted me on the nineteenth of August. I gave him some advice which doesn't matter, then he returned on the sixteenth of September. I filed his suit on the same day. Does that answer the question?'

Gently briefly inclined his head.

'I know what number four will be, but I'd better let you ask it.'

'Who was the co-respondent in the case?'

'Yes, that's the jackpot question. He was Raymond John Heslington of Hadrian's Villa, Wimbledon Common.'

Sharp glanced surprisedly at Evans. He had said something very powerful in Welsh . . .

CHAPTER SIX

'WOULD YOU REALLY credit it, man? Could any case be such a bastard?'

They had gone to the Cheshire for their elevenses; Gently, Evans, and the driver. About them, dallying over coffee, sat the regular clientele: City men, law men and pressmen, the last with a speculative eye for Gently. It was a relaxed and somnolent atmosphere of refreshment and conversation, and Gently was relaxing: Evans had forgotten how it was done. The lawyer's revelation had stunned him. He seemed unequal to exchanging ideas. He could only, between blank reveries, express his feelings in exclamations. The driver was exercising his professional phlegm and drank his coffee in strict anonymity.

'I mean we're never sure of anything. It's up and down the whole time. A step forward and a step back, that's the way of it, in a nutshell . . .'

Gently nodded, not really listening though taking it in at the same time. A step forward and a step back . . . ? It was more like the treading of an intricate dance measure. And what did it signify, that figure which the movements sought to describe: was it the guiltiness of an adulterer, of an unhinged husband, or of something quite different? For look at it how you would, a perplexing dichotomy was showing. The facts divided themselves into groups though the groups were closely linked to each other. On the one hand were Fleece and Kincaid, dancing their diabolical duo, as though between them lay a malignant secret which drew them on to violent ends; and on the other was the dance of the antlers, no less sinister in its setting, separate and several from the first yet counterpointing it all the way. Kincaid had appeared: Fleece had gone to Wales. Fleece may have married Paula Kincaid; Kincaid may have discovered it. Heslington loved Mrs Fleece, may have loved her husband's property. Fleece attempts to get a divorce, Fleece is pushed over Snowdon. Kincaid is inexplicably on the spot, Heslington is there quite explicably. And from Llanberis, from someone, comes the news to Mrs Fleece Kincaid's hideout; over and above which strange background shufflings from the father-figure of Metropolitan Electric. Two themes, yet interacting in a unified spectacle: one climax, but separately danced to by two diversely motivated principals . . .

Gently paused before this picture: a slender consequence had suddenly struck him. For hadn't they conferred on one occasion, those two apparently isolated dancers? They had; it was public knowledge. It had happened during the original notoriety. Heslington had paid Kincaid a visit and had afterwards been loud in the Kincaid cause. Was it credible for them to have conspired together, one to act and one to take the blame? Heslington to clear himself by bearing witness, Kincaid to take the risk of a weak persecution? But no, their motives could not be reconciled, supposing Mrs Fleece to be Paula Kincaid; and if she were not then they were back with Everest for Kincaid's motive to do the deed. And was that enough? Gently had his doubts. Kincaid had never shown signs of grudge-bearing. On the contrary, he'd seemed unconscious that any injury had been done to him . . .

But Kincaid had appeared and both he and Fleece had gone to Wales: that was the point to which one kept returning. Their visits might still have to be connected to be shown more than a coincidence, but on the acute balance of Gently's instinct they levelled one with the other. And what else had been reported from Wales, apart from the circumstances of the tragedy? One thing only, a shy pirouette on the very edge of the ensemble. The witness who had first reported having seen Kincaid had left a false name and address, and one suggesting that he was resident in or familiar with the district. Could this obscure individual have been the reason for the visits? It seemed unlikely; but it was all there was, and Gently didn't like to pass it over.

He drank the last of his coffee.

'I'd like you to give Caernarvon a ring. I want to know if they've traced Fleece's movements and if they've found that witness.'

'Do you think he was Kincaid's missus in disguise, man?'

88

Gently chuckled. 'I'd like to think it was possible. Also, in view of Fleece's visits, we'd better increase the scope of the inquiries. All the district about Caernarvon: give your man what we got from Bemmells.'

Evans nodded. 'Then do we pick up Heslington?'

'No . . . I'm not quite ready for him yet. I want a little more background material. I think we'll go for our chat with Overton.'

They collected their car and drove to the convenient Bow Street, but Evans drew a blank in his talk with Caernarvon. Fleece had stayed with the club party during their weekend in Wales, and no information had come in yet relating to 'Basil Gwynne-Davies'. Inquiries had been made at Bangor, at the University College, but if any students had been adrift on Monday it was unknown to the authorities. Evans gave the new instructions and rang off with a shrug. He was resigned, the gesture said. Out of Wales could come no comfort.

Richard Overton was an architect and he lived in Bayswater, but he had an office in Bedford Place only a short distance from Bow Street. It was contained in a terrace house, a gracious segment of Bloomsbury, its brickwork seedily metropolitan but its paintwork professionally gay. Overton's studio was on the first floor. It was a large room lined with shelves and racks. It contained a vast table, some bentwood chairs and a pair of mechanized-looking drawing boards, and it smelled of paper and rubbers and indian ink and cigarette smoke. When they were announced Overton was busy at an elevation on one of the boards. He extended a warning finger towards them while he drew a line with a metal ruler. Then, after a moment of appraisal, he turned to them with a smile.

'A block of flats for the L.C.C., or so I hope in my innocence. School of Gibberd, I fear me. But I know better than to be original.'

He shook hands with a warm grasp and pulled out chairs for them to sit on; a dark-haired, dark-eyed man of medium height, his build powerful, his complexion sallow. He had a boldly retroussé nose, a rounded chin, and a wide mouth. His voice was pleasant and his manner ingratiating. He had given his age as forty-six.

'It's too much to hope that you've come here with a commission?'

'Not today, I'm afraid.' Gently returned his smile.

'That's a pity. I've some pet ideas about a contemporary police station. A courtyard model with glass doors and a measure of liberty for detainees. Do you think it would catch on?'

'You could circularize the Watch committees.'

'No, thank you. That's a polite way of telling me to go to hell. But it will come, one fine day. After they've done it in Stockholm. That's the only official channel for getting architecture into England.'

He offered them cigarettes from a packet, then tapped and lit one himself. He didn't seem overly curious about the object of their visit. He had a completely social attitude as though content with their bare company, and it was easy to see how he would gravitate naturally to the post of a club official.

Gently said: 'You'll have had time to think about this

Kincaid question now. Can you give me a straight answer – is the fellow genuine or not?'

Overton laughed. 'You don't catch me. But I can give you a straight contingency. And nothing will ever make me go further than that.'

'What's your contingency.?'

'It's this.' Overton's lids sank, narrowing his eyes. 'I'm half convinced – three-quarters convinced – that Kincaid is who he claims to be. But I've yet to be convinced that a man can descend Everest unaided, and any identification I make is contingent on that being proved possible. If I'm asked in court I shall answer just that.'

Gently nodded acknowledgement. 'You've considered his story about the Tibetans?'

'I certainly have. And furthermore, I've done some research on it. It's quite true that there's a tribe who make the Yeti a totem, they're called the Yashmaks and they live in the foothills of the eastern Himalayas. They're secretive and superstitious, they live in valleys at a high altitude, and they are believed by their neighbours to hold communication with the Yeti. Which is all very encouraging and supports Kincaid's story wonderfully: except that he, like myself, could have read about it in London; and except for the fact that on his oxygen supply he could scarcely have reached the South Summit, let alone any point where he might have met the Yashmaks. They couldn't have got on the South Col without the assistance of oxygen.'

'That can be ruled out as impossible?'

'Pretty well, I should say. Though some amazing feats have been performed on Everest without oxygen. But nobody has climbed the South Col except from the Western Cwm, so it's barely possible for an easy route to it to exist to the east. Then the Yashmaks might have got up there. But not as far as the South Summit.'

'Suppose Kincaid had got a little lower and the Yashmaks a little higher . . . ?'

Overton shook his head, laughing. 'Now you're entering the realm of miracles. I'm allowing Kincaid to be superhuman to descend as far as the South Summit, but after that, with no oxygen, he couldn't have lasted for very long. It wasn't a scramble in Wales, you know. The conditions were at the limit of human endurance.'

'Yes . . . I see.' Gently pondered. 'But suppose I let you into a secret. Suppose I told you that Kincaid's story checks back to India – to Kathmandu?'

Overton stared. 'Is that a fact?'

'Yes. We've vetted it back to there.'

Overton whistled very softly. 'Then it's a bit of a poser,' he said.

He got up. He took one or two steps about the room, his hands in his pockets, his head slanted forward. He stopped in front of a wall map and appeared to study it for a moment. Then he said, not turning:

'I told you I was three-quarters convinced.'

'He'd be changed, of course.'

'He has. He's changed enormously. More than one would have thought possible, though you have to allow for what he's been through. And then his eyes haven't changed . . . his voice . . . his head: even back there at the Asterbury he gave me an uncomfortable feeling. And he knew a lot about Tibet, more than any of us did. Though there were gaps in his knowledge when it came to the expedition. But that's explainable too: he'd have no reason to remember it much; while we, on the other hand, have never let the subject rest . . .'

'But you still think it impossible for him to have got down off Everest?'

Overton made a gliding step, then turned in their direction again.

'You're making it difficult,' he said. 'You're making it damnably difficult. I've given you my reasons for thinking so and they're one hundred per cent sound, sitting here, in Bloomsbury, half the world away from Everest. But I'm shaken, I have to admit it. Kincaid was always a curiosity. If a miracle had to happen to someone, he'd be the man I'd put my money on.'

'Are you sure that a miracle was necessary?'

'Confound it, yes. Let me save my face! It would have needed all of a miracle, and from that position I won't be shifted.'

'So you agree that Kincaid is Kincaid?'

'You've got me practically taking an oath on it.'

Gently smiled on him benevolently. 'Later,' he said. 'We'll dispense with that now.'

To the visible impatience of Evans, who had ceased to think in terms of Kincaid, Gently now switched from the identity angle to the beginnings of that tiresome expedition. He went leisurely about it, sparing no pains, drawing out detail after detail; leading Overton to talk freely, circumstantially, revealingly. For the moment he seemed to have forgotten about Heslington.

'Who first suggested the expedition?'

Overton was seated again now. Both he and Gently had reversed their chairs and were conversing across the backs of them.

'I couldn't tell you. It was one of those things. You know how it is when you're young and foolish? A lot of you with similar tastes get together, then out of the blue an idea is born. It doesn't signify how impossible it is, in fact that's the essence of the phenomenon: you dream up something wildly improbable, and then it grows, and then you find yourself doing it. Well, that was the way of our expedition. Some cotton-headed youngsters dreamed up a stunt. And at the drop of a hat it had stopped being a stunt, and suddenly we were committed to it in deadly earnest.'

'But didn't you need money for a thing like that?'

'How right you are. An astronomical sum of money. And I was the innocent they picked on to raise it, so I can give you the details of our sordid transactions. First I went to the Royal Geographical Society, who are usual Maecenases of Everest Expeditions. I dated their secretary and I talked to him for an hour. It makes me blush when I look back on that.'

'Did it do any good?'

'No. It didn't raise a ha'penny. They said we were too inexperienced, and they were absolutely right. But it was no good telling us, it only roused our determination, and being an unscrupulous little cad I gave the story to the *Echo*. Then we did get some offers. I had whole sackfuls of correspondence. People wanted us to test everything from army battledress to malted milk tablets. In the end we got the best part of our stores and equipment for nothing, but so far no money. And that was the thing we needed most.'

'But you got that too, eventually.'

Overton gave his little laugh. 'Yes, we did. And when you learn how you'll think I should be the last person to sneer at miracles. It simply came through the post – a banker's order for ten thousand pounds; there was no warning, no fanfares, no conditions, and no name. It had a note enclosed with it to say what it was for and praising our spirit of adventure, but expressing a wish to remain anonymous. We don't know to this day who patronized our expedition. We could only thank him through the Press, and carry a flag to represent him.'

'That was a very large sum to be made over so lightly.'

'Yes, wasn't it? The man would need to be a Docker or somebody.'

'Who signed the banker's order?'

'Oh, a firm of solicitors in the city. We tried to pump them of course. But they wouldn't breathe a word.'

'What were their names?'

'I don't remember, though I could probably find out. Is it important?'

Gently shrugged. 'Yes . . . I feel we ought to know it.'

'I'll go through my files at home. I'm pretty certain to have a note of it.'

Gently lit his pipe, thinking, still feeding Overton with questions. Could it fail to be of significance, this second mysterious provision of money? Someone had financed the expedition. Someone had set up Fleece in business. Were the odds very long against them having been the same person? And if this were so, what had been their object, and who could afford such Croesusian tactics? One thought immediately of Mr Stanley and of the industrial empire lying behind him. Was he the mover? Gently considered. He'd checked on Stanley the previous evening. He was a widower; he'd married the daughter of a well-known sporting brewer. She had died in nineteen-fifty and there could be no ambiguity in her case, but supposing the plot had lain elsewhere, in some latent threat to the giant firm? And Fleece, on two occasions, had tapped that potential, exploiting a dangerous secret he'd learned; and with the return of Kincaid had tried again, but this time had lost his life in the attempt. Could that be the pattern of it – the Nemesis which waited for Fleece on Snowdon?

'Fleece led the expedition, didn't he?'

'Yes, he was the eldest member of the party. He'd been to the Alps for several years and he was a sound man on ice.'

'Was it he who suggested the expedition?'

'Not a bit of it. At first he was one of the sceptics.

96

But then, when things were hanging in the balance, he seemed to change his mind and grow enthusiastic. That was a turning point, I don't mind telling you. It occurred just before we received the money. Fleece had a flair for organization, and his coming in like that gave us all fresh heart.'

'Did you know him well at that time?'

'I suppose I did, in a sort of way. We both belonged to the Fell and Rock Climbers Club. Most of the expedition were members of that.'

'What was your personal impression of Fleece?'

Overton lit a fresh cigarette before replying. 'Personally, I didn't take to him much.' He inhaled once or twice. 'But he had lots of good qualities. He made an excellent leader, and we couldn't have done without him.'

'What were some of his bad qualities?'

'Oh, nothing really bad. He was a little chilly, that's all, and inclined to be calculating. Rather liked his own way and didn't care how he got it. But remember that's speaking personally, so don't hold it against him.'

'Was he friendly with Kincaid? They both worked for the same firm.'

'He was neither friendly or unfriendly, as far as I can recall it.'

'Did he visit Kincaid's house?'

'I don't know. I shouldn't think so. He was the lone wolf type and didn't much go in for visiting. But I was pally with Kincaid myself, he was such a peculiar and uncommon bird. And the oddest thing he ever did was getting hitched to Paula Blackman.'

'Why do you say that?'

'Why?' Overton closed one eye and nodded. 'She was a prize packet, was Paula. One of the marry-go-round brigade.'

'A good-looker, I've heard.'

'She had beauty, and more. She was a girl with ambitions, quite the wrong sort for Kincaid. I suppose he talked her into marrying him because he had the gift of the gab. But I'll never believe it could have lasted, not if it had been put to the test.'

'She had a roving eye, had she?'

'No; not especially that. I never did see anything that struck me as suspicious. But it was her type, you know, she was the edible social-climber. And Kincaid was no summit for ambitions of that sort.'

'Who broke to her the news of Kincaid's death?'

'Heaven knows. I tried to see her, but she'd vanished when I got back.'

'Would you know her again if you met her?'

'Well . . . I might and I might not. I can't honestly visualize her features, but something about her might jog my memory.'

Silently Gently produced the photograph he had borrowed from Mrs Fleece. He handed it to Overton, who accepted it with interest. He took his time over examining it, holding the photograph at different distances, but one could tell from his expression that no penny had dropped.

'I'm sorry, but I don't seem to recognize this lady.'

Gently retrieved it. 'How many of the others had met Paula Kincaid?' he asked.

Overton considered a moment. 'One has to bear in mind that Kincaid wasn't terribly popular. There was probably only myself and Fleece – oh yes, and Ray Heslington.'

At that name Evans perked up, but Gently was only nodding his head indifferently.

'Good,' he said. 'Now I'd like to run through again what happened on Monday . . .'

Gently had lit his pipe and both the others were smoking incessantly, filling the studio, in spite of its spaciousness, with a heavy miasma of smoke. Below them in Bedford Place the traffic droned a restless litany, and the weak noonday sun cast its shadows towards Russell Square. London: the rampired heart of it, protected by miles of sunned, sooty walls; a world away from the swept helm of Everest and the choughs that echoed their cries by Snowdon . . .

'Fleece was wearing a red windcheater, so we had no difficulty in picking him out. It was sunny, with a cool southerly breeze, and the visibility was a hundred per cent. We started off around ten-ish, intending to take the ascent easily, most of us choosing the lower route down by the llyns and the old copper mine. Heslington and Fleece preferred the Pyg Track and Heslington set out a little in advance. There are two or three paths which begin that route. Fleece chose a different one to Ray's.'

Before him Gently had a large-scale map of the Snowdon theatre, a fierce brown-tinted piece of cartography full of swirling lines and fretted teeth.

Overton pointed to the chopped lines which indicated the tracks which had been taken: desperate thoroughfares they looked, fit for goats and sheep only.

'The Snowdon group is a rough horseshoe stretching from the Lliwedd round to Crib Goch, a pretty useful lot of rocks taking one with another. It encloses Llyd Llydaw there, which is crossed by a causeway, and in a lap higher up is the Glaslyn, which drains into Llydaw. Now the Pyg Track runs here, along the footslopes of Crib Goch, and as you can see it's a good deal shorter than the llyns route. In fact I was just pulling up to the Glaslyn when I caught sight of Heslington; and by then he was on this ridge joining Crib-y-ddysgl to the Wyddfa.'

'Are you positive that it was Heslington?' Gently interrupted.

Overton hesitated, his eyes distancing. 'I thought it was Heslington at the time. True, he was wearing nothing distinctive, just the usual rambler's trim, but my automatic reaction was "There's Ray up ahead." Then, after I reached the Glaslyn, I saw Fleece's windcheater on the Zigzags, which are the series of traverses here stretching from the Glaslyn to the top of the ridge. I waited for the others to come up with me before I started on the Zigzags, and by that time Fleece had gained the ridge and gone up along it towards the summit. I saw the windcheater show once or twice where there were gaps among the rock-rims.

'Now try to picture this if you can. You're at the foot of the ridge inside the horseshoe. It lifts up above you about twelve hundred feet, all fairly steep going over loose rock and outcrops. Closing you in on the right is Crib-y-ddysgl and Crib Goch, and on the left stand the Wyddfa and the Lliwedd rocks. The Wyddfa falls away in a cliff almost sheer down to the Glaslyn, about fifteen hundred feet without footing enough for a fly. The summit cairn is out of sight. It stands a few yards back from the edge.

'Hold that picture. When the others arrived I continued my way up the Zigzags, which are a straightforward section, though they tend to be exhausting; and I reckoned I was better than halfway up, about on a level with Crib Goch, when I heard that frightful cry and saw Fleece come plunging down the cliff.'

Overton broke off; a peculiar expression was on his rounded, olive face. His brown eyes glittered. They seemed to stare through the map at which they were directed.

'It's something I'll never forget, my God. It's difficult to give any real impression of it. He seemed to be falling so very slowly, as though he'd got no weight at all . . . And he didn't kick or lash with his arms; he just fell, and kept on falling. And those cliffs have a terrible echo. I can't get his cry out of my ears.

'I heard him strike, but I had turned my head: I couldn't watch it, it was something obscene. Once, twice, and then he began rolling. He came to rest a few hundred yards from the llyn. But here's something I didn't give you in my statement, I was too confused at the time I made it. I remember hearing something before the cry, as though Fleece had first called or shouted at someone.'

Gently looked up from the map, his mind slowly refocusing: out of the riven Welsh sky, away from the rocky cockpit of Snowdon.

'Did you hear what he shouted?'

'Yes . . . I think I did. It was "No—!" – like that, as though he'd seen his danger. I may be rationalizing, of course, so I wouldn't like to be too certain, but I did hear the sound. It made me start to raise my head.'

'Where was he when you first saw him?'

'He was just below the summit. Falling outwards and flattening, as though he'd gone over backwards.'

'Did you see anyone else up there?'

'No. I wouldn't have forgotten that. But then I wasn't looking for them . . . my eyes were fixed on something else.'

'Carry on with your statement.'

Overton lit another cigarette. He drew on it heavily before continuing, driving the smoke through his nostrils.

'After it happened . . . it knocked the steam out of me, I came over weak as a child. At the first shock I couldn't believe it, it was as though I had watched it in a dream. But something had to be done, he might even still have been alive. People have taken tumbles like that and lived to dine out on it afterwards. So I bawled down to the others: I don't remember what I said: then I kept on going up like a madman to get at the telephone in the café.'

'Did you meet anyone coming down? Down the ridge towards Llanberis?'

'No, I didn't. But if they were quick they might

102

have passed before I arrived there. And he was on the railway, too, wasn't he? The railway is cut in below the track. The first person I saw was Heslington: he was coming round the café, eating an apple.'

'What did he say?'

'He wanted to know what all the panic was about. I was sweating, you can imagine, and just about winded. When I told him it gave him a shaking, I remember him goggling at me over the apple; I think he went up to take a look while I was breaking open a window. I phoned the police down in Llanberis. They rang the people at Pen-y-Gwryd. Mountain Rescue arrived within the hour and the police about half an hour later. Two of our blokes had worked across to Fleece, but . . . I don't have to tell you. You've seen the report.'

Overton, with Heslington, had waited at the summit where they were joined at intervals by the others. Heslington had seemed rather quiet and had held back from the conversation. During the interval before the police came they had all gone up to inspect the summit, but according to Overton, who'd been one of the first, they'd found nothing there to account for the tragedy. Nobody, he thought, had gone on to the cairn, nor had anybody lingered about the spot. After some questioning, they'd descended to Llanberis and had given their statements at the police station.

'What was the impression you formed of the business?'

Gently had folded his arms over the back of the chair; his pipe stuck forgotten from the corner of his mouth and his chin rested squarely on the arms in front of him.

'You mean at the time?'

'Yes. Waiting on the summit.'

'It was confused . . . an inexplicable accident. When you've had such a shock you're at a loss, you're not logical. You feel you can't rely on things making sense.'

'You knew that Heslington had been up there, didn't you?'

'Yes, I did . . . but I simply didn't connect it. I know Ray well. I've known him for years. I may have thought it would look bad for him, but anything else was too improbable.'

'Yet you knew he was scarcely a friend of Fleece's.'

'Yes, I knew it.' Overton rocked his shoulders as though to shrug away the imputation. 'Now it doesn't matter, so I don't mind telling you, but they almost came to blows over the Kincaid question. But that didn't affect the issue. I never doubted Ray for a moment. When he told me he hadn't seen Fleece it was good enough. I knew he hadn't.'

'Though you had heard of the divorce pending?'

'Divorce? What divorce?'

'Fleece's divorce of his wife. Citing Heslington as co-respondent.'

A silence followed. It was difficult to mistake Overton's look of alarmed incredulity. His cigarette was held stationary, he sat perfectly still on his chair. For several moments he remained dumb, his eyes large and disbelieving, then they tightened and he made a little flicking motion with the cigarette.

'Now I see where we stand. And I can tell you it makes no difference. I know Ray. If you suspect him, you're being less intelligent than I thought you.'

'I understand.'

Gently remembered his pipe; he straightened it out and put a match to it. He gave a side glance to Evans as though inviting him to try a question. The Welshman sat stolidly, however, blowing and drawing at his cheeks, and after a puff or two Gently added:

'If we can go back to Everest for a moment . . .'

'That's what really counts, isn't it?' Overton's relief was unconcealed. He drew in a grateful lungful of smoke and let it trickle through his lips.

'I'd like to know if you can remember how that final assault came about. Was it according to your schedule, or was the schedule interrupted?'

Overton nodded. 'I can guess what you're driving at there. And the answer is yes. The schedule was definitely interrupted. As we'd planned it, Ray and myself were to have had the first crack at it, with Fleece and Kincaid as the support party if our attempt failed. But the weather looked like breaking up – did, in fact, the next day – and Fleece altered the arrangement so that he and Kincaid went first. He gave his greater experience as the reason. Which was sound enough as far as it went.'

'I'm angling for impressions again. How did you feel about Fleece's story?'

'Well . . . I felt bound to accept it, though I thought he'd acted irresponsibly. In no circumstances ought he to have let Kincaid continue alone.'

'What about Kincaid's version; assuming that to be the true one?'

Overton shrugged. 'Assuming it's true, there can be no doubt about that. Fleece was intending to get rid of him. You can call it what you like.'

'Could they have been separated by accident?'

'Never. They went off on a rope.'

'So that if Kincaid released himself, the rope would be left behind with Fleece?'

'Yes, that follows.'

'And did he bring a rope back with him?'

Overton's stare was blank for a second, then it snapped into a sudden intelligence as the inference clicked home.

'My God, no. We were one short. There was one missing the next morning.'

'And it wasn't Heslington's and yours?'

'It damned well wasn't. It was Fleece and Kincaid's.'

CHAPTER SEVEN

I T HAD STARTED to mizzle again as a matter of course; that sunshine had been far too fragile; now it had relapsed into a suffused presence behind the ceiling of steady grey. The shadows of buildings were smoothed and softened and the presence of the buildings strangely enlarged, while the railway smell of London streets had sharpened until it pressed upon the consciousness. At Evans's request they had lunched at a Corner House, a murmuring hall of communal eating; and now they were driving out to Wimbledon, retracing their route of the day before. Evans was deep in a midday paper: his sombre mood had become almost a sulk. The matter of the rope had failed to stir his enthusiasm, it was a frivolous detail, it was almost academic.

'But it happened all that time ago, man.' During lunch he had condescended to discuss it. 'Kincaid's forgotten it, if he ever understood. That's plain enough now, and I ought to have my head tested.'

'It gives a sound enough motive, taken together with the circumstances.'

'Aye, so I thought. And you've proved me wrong.'

'And for the first time it enables us to link Kincaid with Kincaid.'

'That's bloody magnificent. You job is done, man.'

So Gently had let it drop, though he felt absurdly pleased with himself. It had been no mean feat, this slipping of a lassoo over Kincaid. A lot of talent had been loosed on it before Gently came on the scene, and up till that moment nothing tangible had emerged from the research. But now it had. That missing rope flashed an unmistakable positive. It underwrote Kincaid's story with a persuasive flourish. The shadowy past has been penetrated and the shadowy present grown more distinct: this might be only a first step, but it suggested that further steps were possible. And who knew even yet what the value of identifying Kincaid might be? The spotlight had shifted on to Heslington, but it was a purely circumstantial spotlight . . .

Evans lowered his paper and gave the Thames a dirty look, but he raised it again as they crawled through Putney. The Welsh inspector had no more doubts, he was seeing the case in black and white; in that curious dance of death his attention was fixed on Raymond Heslington. But Kincaid was still there, he still held the centre of the stage. He remained the dancer whose appearance had set the ballet in motion. Was it possible to dismiss him now as an accidental subsidiary, a monumental introduction to a commonplace finale? Gently involuntarily shook his head. He couldn't credit that, yet. Now, before he had seen Heslington, he could affirm that his mind was still open. In an hour it might be different, this was what they were going to discover; but as they drove towards Wimbledon the balance was level, though tremulous.

Hadrian's Villa, Heslington's house, was sited actually on the Common, and appeared as a white flat-topped building partly hidden by a grove of birches. It had a courtyard which was enclosed by high pantile-capped walls, and these were pierced by a round-arched gateway and by occasional unglazed windows. The driver parked before the gateway and the two of them got out. Through the wrought-iron gate, which bore an imperial eagle, they could see a formal garden and a colonnade. The paths of the garden were of zigzagged brick, and in the centre stood the statue of a youth, in bronze; the colonnade was reached by a shallow flight of steps and its tiled roof was supported by short, slab-top pillars. Over the gateway was a round stone plaque. Its inscription read: HAD-RIANVS AVGVSTVS.

There was a bell-pull and Gently tugged at it, producing a distant, melodious chime. After an interval a door was opened and a woman came across to the gate. They both stared at her in amazement; she was a surprise for Wimbledon Common; she was dressed in a voluminous scarlet robe which was tucked in at the waist with a belt of leather. On her feet she had drawstring sandals and her hair was piled beneath a copper ring. She was about fifty and had rather hard features. She eyed them coldly but without embarrassment.

'You wanted something?'

Her voice spoiled the illusion. It was a voice from the wrong side of Aldgate Pump.

'We want to speak to Mr Heslington. We are C.I.D. officers.'

'Oh, I see. It's about that, is it? You'd better come in while I go and tell him. Mr Heslington's a bit particular; he doesn't like people to come disturbing him.'

She closed the gate with a slight slam and led them over to the colonnade, her long robe swishing at every step and her sandals shuffling on the bricks. When she'd left them their eyes met and their shoulders lifted in unison. There was no commenting on this: one could only exchange a gesture! Gently glanced round the courtyard. It was all of a piece with the general theme; various round-arched, stump-pillared out-buildings, some miniature holm-oaks and minor statuary. He noticed a pair of modern folding doors.

'Take a look into the garage, will you?'

Evans sneaked over and tried to open the doors, but they were apparently locked and he was obliged to squint through the window. He returned.

'So what does he keep there. A couple of chariots for the Common?'

'No, man. A Ford Anglia. And a green-and-cream Austin-Healey.'

'Then where the devil—?' Gently was beginning, when the return of the housekeeper interrupted him. She threw a look at Evans which suggested that she had witnessed his manoeuvre.

'Mr Heslington says he'll see you, if you'll *kindly* step inside. It's the second door on the right.'

She flounced rustlingly away.

A passage ran the length of the house as an interior parallel to the colonnade and its floor was paved with mosaic in a pattern of red and white. Gently tapped at the door, which was painted apple-green, and on hearing a response turned the bronze claw handle. It was like straying on to a theatre set. The room beyond was awe-inspiring. It was some fifteen feet in height and perhaps twenty feet square. The walls were panelled with rusty marble, framed by inlays of alabaster, and a frieze of the same material was rendered with formalized designs in colour. The floor was bare and of warm, veined stone, with a rich mosaic in the centre, and the only furniture was a marble table with gilded legs and lion-claw feet. The room possessed an antechamber on the side opposite to the door. This opened into a conservatory in which grew a vine and some potted shrubs. It also contained some more useful furnishings, a table in bronze, a bench and a couch, and it was here that Heslington stood waiting for them: clad – it was inevitable – in a purple toga.

'*Tempori parendum*. Come in and sit down.'

He was a man who, surprisingly, looked well in a toga. His age was forty-four and his height about five feet ten; he was lean but broad in the shoulder, and his shoulders sloped gracefully. But there was nothing Roman in his features unless it was the slight hook of the nose; he had reddish hair, flecked with grey, hazel eyes and a full beard. His complexion was fresh and his teeth uneven but good, and he spoke in a deep tone with a good deal of resonance. He nodded to Evans but didn't shake hands.

'I thought you'd settled this business, Inspector. I didn't expect you to lug me back to it from the public baths in Pompeii.'

Evans looked startled. 'From where was it you said, sir?'

'The public baths in Pompeii.' Heslington pointed to the paper-strewn table. 'I'd just written myself in. I write books, you know. And I was deep in the baths when Mrs Vincent came to announce you. But never mind, I'm out now; I'm busy towelling my hair. So if the twentieth century has questions, let the second century hear them.'

He did it well, but not well enough to conceal his uneasiness, nor to control the challenging glance which he flashed at Gently. The twentieth century was probably closer than the second century liked to admit, and stood in danger of closing the gap with less than senatorial ceremony.

'This is Superintendent Gently, sir. He's assisting me in the case.' Evans was curt. He stepped back a pace to leave no doubt who was the principal.

'Really?' Heslington surveyed Gently again. Now it was with a touch of boredom. 'I hope I can do something for him besides repeating repetitions. Would you be interested in archaeological reconstruction, Superintendent?'

Gently hunched non-commitally. 'I'm always interested in reconstructions.'

'You stand on the site and in the *triclinium* of an Anglo-Roman villa. The Emperor Hadrian's I maintain, though I fail to carry a majority.'

'My reconstructions are more modern.'

'After Rome the field is plebeian.'

'All the same, it has its points. I've a present interest in cars.'

'You've come to the wrong person, I'm afraid.'

Gently shook his head. 'I don't think so. I'm wondering how you run an Austin-Healey in addition to the car you've officially taxed.'

Heslington's eyes hardened a little but he gave no other reaction. He said: 'I fail to see how that can interest you. I may have hired or borrowed the car.'

'From whom did you borrow it?'

'Is that really your business?'

'I'm asking you because you're handy. But I could put the same question to Sarah Fleece.'

Now there was a reaction, a burning spot on each cheekbone. After a moment's silence Heslington turned from them and threw himself down on a stool by the table. His toga made the action dramatic, it was at one with the theatrical tone of the setting; a declamation in blank verse might with propriety have followed the move. Gently hesitated, then selected the bronze bench for a seat. Evans chose the couch with an equal diffidence.

'Just precisely what are you after?' His patronizing condescension had come to an end. His face was bitter. The lines to the mouth were drawn deep and tight. 'I don't have to answer your questions. I've given you my

113

account of Monday. You've made an arrest, so what's your object in coming scandal-mongering here?'

A smile loitered on Gently's lips: that line of appeal was really getting too common! 'You can call it routine,' he replied. 'We're finding this an unusual case.'

'It may be unusual, but it isn't doubtful, so you've no reason to be offensive. Hound Kincaid if you want to, but don't come here hounding me.'

'You're certain that Kincaid is our man?'

'Isn't it a fact that you've charged him with it? It's an open and shut case, to use your questionable expression. And I'm sorry for it, too. He's a remarkable man is Kincaid. The whole affair makes me sick and I'd like to forget it ever happened.'

'You're quite satisfied about the motive. About it's being an act of revenge?'

'Yes, I am. I was there. I know what happened on Everest.'

'You knew that Fleece intended to get rid of him?'

'I knew it after I'd heard his story. It made me remember a whole lot of things which I'd paid no attention to at the time. But I saw their significance after I'd talked to Kincaid. It made the whole thing as clear as daylight. I understood the delays and the switching of teams, and all Fleece's little manoeuvrings to get Kincaid on his rope. You don't have to worry about the poor devil's motive.'

'Why did Fleece do it, do you think?'

'I don't know and I don't want to. Finding it out was like stumbling on a midden in your drawing room.

114

Till then the affair had a certain nobility, it was tragic but left us with an inspiration; then it turned into an ugly mess which seemed to dirty us too. I always knew that Fleece was a blackguard but after that my soul loathed him. And I told him so to his face. I did have that satisfaction.'

'In fact, it nearly came to violence.'

Heslington checked himself before replying. He said evenly: 'You must have read my statement. I said there that I didn't like him.'

'That's not quite the same is it? As loathing a man with your soul?'

'It was sufficient for the occasion and the officialese of the document.'

'Wouldn't it be true to say that you're glad he's dead?'

'It might or might not be true. But I don't remember having said it.'

His eyes met Gently's steadily and with the hint of a challenge again; it was the look of a man either conscious of his innocence or of the strength of his position. Which was it? With a man like Heslington it was not easy to tell. A bit of a crank he might be, but he was not without strength of character. Gently's gaze strayed towards the conservatory.

'I'll put a hypothetical case,' he said. 'Suppose Kincaid told the truth in his statement. Suppose it wasn't him you saw on the railway?'

'But it was.'

'Did you recognize him?'

'I'm nearly certain. It was about his build.'

'The supporting evidence is not strong. And this is the first time you've made an identification.'

'But I didn't know he was in the district, not when I made my statement. At the time nobody was further from my thoughts than Kincaid. But I remembered clearly what I'd seen, the height and build of the fellow, and after Overton had identified the cigarette-case I realized at once who it must have been. And I said so then.'

'Wasn't that wisdom after the event?'

'Perhaps. I found it convincing enough.'

'But would a jury find it convincing, when so much depends on your evidence? We'll carry the hypothesis a stage further, as Kincaid's Counsel will certainly do: suppose your statement was a false one, wouldn't your identification seem a little convenient?'

'Why should my statement have been a false one?'

'Hypothetically, to avert suspicion.'

'From me. You mean that?'

'From the lover of Mrs Fleece.'

Again the tell-tale spots welled up over the areas below the eyes. Heslington jerked bolt upright, disarranging the flowing folds of the toga. 'Who says . . . who dares . . . ?' He found it hard to check this time. It took him a struggle of several seconds before he succeeded in becoming calm.

'I deny that allegation. I completely deny it.'

'But taken as a hypothesis it could be useful to Kincaid's Counsel. Suppose it were true: suppose it could be shown that Fleece had begun divorce proceedings: given that Fleece is a rich man, where would that line of reasoning finish?'

'There are no grounds for such a hypothesis!'

'But there were grounds for Fleece's divorce. It was filed on 16th September. On the day when Mrs Fleece booked a room in the Suffolk.'

'Oh . . . God!'

It was still theatrical. He slumped forward heavily over the table, a thrown-out arm scattering papers which floated gently to the stone floor. Evans collected and returned them, but Heslington held his pose unmoved. It was photogenic; it might have served for some dramatic historical painting.

'Have you any comment to make on that?'

He turned his outstretched hand palm upwards.

'Do you dispute it?'

'*Humanum est errare*. The truth should be beyond dispute.'

'Then you see where it leads us?'

'I see. And I tremble.'

'Yet you haven't any comment.'

'Ought I to have, without my lawyer?'

He drew back slowly from the table, allowing his hand to drag across it; letting it stay there, the arm stiff, while he extended his other hand in a gesture.

'Listen to me. I admit it all, I won't abase myself by denying it. I had a presentiment of why you were here, though I did my best to deceive myself. But your hypothesis is false: as false as a late Italian bust. I've told the truth about what happened on Snowdon, and in the name of justice you've got to believe me. Kincaid was there. I'm sorry for him, but he was there. And he had his reasons.'

★ ★ ★

Now it was impressive; he had suddenly transcended the air of theatre that surrounded him, producing a hard note of conviction from the soft paste of histrionics. Though he remained with hand outstretched like an amateur Mark Antony, it didn't detract from the overall impression of his sincerity. Was it genuine, or was he treating them to a superior level of art? Gently studied him with interest, his professional palate tickled. Now Heslington dropped the hand, crisply, letting it hang beside him: signalling almost for the supporting dialogue which had waited on his pause. Gently accepted the cue.

'We'll set the hypothesis aside for the moment. When did you meet Mrs Fleece, and how long has it been going on?'

Heslington's hand stirred feebly. 'Do we have to go into that? I've admitted the fact, and it's not flattering. Surely the details are unimportant.'

'Didn't you know her before she married him?'

'No, I didn't. Or it wouldn't have happened. I met her first two years ago, through some mutual friends. The Rogers, of Surbiton.'

'Didn't you know her when she lived in Putney?'

'Putney? I never knew she'd lived there.'

'But you used to visit Kincaid in Putney.'

'Suppose I did. That was before the war.'

'And you didn't meet there the present Mrs Fleece?'

'I'm sorry, I didn't. She was never around. You seem to have got hold of the wrong end of the stick. Sarah's home used to be in Kensington.'

'Could you describe Mrs Kincaid to me?'

Heslington's shoulders moved faintly under the toga. If he saw any danger in these questions he was masking his awareness of it immaculately.

'I can't say I remember her very well. She was about Sarah's build, perhaps a little thinner. She'd got red hair, though it could hardly have been natural, and a pale complexion, and a rather nice voice. Have you found her yet, by the way?'

'We have an idea of where to look. But haven't you seen her since those days at Putney?'

'Me? I've never set eyes on her since.'

Gently nodded: he accepted it. The trailing hand had barely flourished. It was conceivable that Heslington was ignorant of Mrs Fleece's antecedents. 'Let's return to Mrs Fleece, whom you met two years ago. Give me those unimportant details which you seem to find unflattering.'

The story was scarcely original, for it had been acted since the beginnings of time. The two had met and had been attracted and had found casual ways of meeting again. She'd used a particular restaurant in town and had visited her friends on a certain day; then one day a friend was discreet, and the casual element had vanished. And they had found it more than an affaire, more than a clandestine excitement. It had brought into each of their lives a springlike fragrance of a youth forgotten. They were lovers; they had been predestined, they had found and recognized each other; neither of them had experienced love before those thrilling, electric moments.

'She married Fleece on the rebound from a girlish

crush of some sort. He was wrong for her, completely wrong. He was cold and emotionless and a bit sadistic. She didn't love him: that was impossible, and all he wanted was a presentable wife. She was there to keep house for him, to give him a background, and to bring up a couple of children.'

She'd been starved for companionship and a little warm affection, a woman who'd married in haste to find that life had misdealt to her. She'd accepted her lot and had been a good wife and mother, but the one half of her was suspended; Fleece had frozen it from the start. Heslington, on the other hand, had seemed a dedicated bachelor. His enthusiasms had excluded him from matrimonial inclinations. During the war he had been in the Navy, where he had experienced some light-hearted affaires, but none of these had left a mark on him or suggested that he should change his state. And these two had come together and the spark had fallen. The girl had wakened in the woman and the boy in the man. A new life had spread before them, a new conception of themselves, a new world, a new age: they had fallen in love.

'To begin with we made all sorts of good resolutions. There were her children to be considered, she was terribly concerned about them. But soon we found that we just couldn't do without each other. It grew worse as time went on. We knew a break would have to come.'

'And Fleece? When did he find out?'

'Fleece knew about it almost from the beginning. One of Sarah's so-called friends must have told him, because he wasn't deceived for long. We knew he knew from the way he treated her. He was full of innuendos and cutting allusions. He gave me to understand that Sarah would never have the children and he practically defied me to get her away without them. He was a sadist, as I told you. He was really enjoying the situation.'

'And that went on for two years.'

'Yes, and he was right, damnably right. Sarah loved me, it was tearing her in two, but she couldn't abandon her children to Fleece. He didn't care, he wasn't fond of them. There was no affection in his nature. They were hers and they looked to her, and she couldn't bear to let them down. It became hellish. We were trapped and there was no way out for us. To give it up was unthinkable, yet her children bound her to this man. And it was no use appealing to him, any more than to a block of stone: less in fact. The block of stone wouldn't have played cat and mouse with us.'

'So that was the impasse his death solved.'

Heslington's look was intensely bitter. 'Yes, it did. And I'm not a hypocrite; I shan't pretend to any regrets. But it wasn't me who did the solving, in spite of all your hypotheses. I'm a beneficiary, that's all. And God have mercy on Kincaid.'

'The benefits are certainly plain enough.' Gently's incredulous sarcasm was cuttable.

'Suppose they are. Does that make me a criminal?' Heslington stared at him, sitting magnificently straight.

'I don't know yet what Fleece was worth, but we can estimate a fair-ish sum. And that of course would have gone down the drain if Fleece had lived to complete his divorce.'

'And you think I cared about that?'

'Why not? It was enough to finance a murder.'

'I've money of my own. I earn as much as Fleece did.'

'Isn't it a coincidence that Fleece should die a fortnight after filing his divorce?'

At last there were signs of a breakthrough: a little sweat had formed on Heslington's forehead. That was honest at all events; one didn't control the activities of sweat glands. He got to his feet.

'Now listen to this! If it's coincidences you're after, tell me why, just give me one reason, why Fleece should file that divorce at all?'

Gently quizzed him through narrowed lids. 'I wouldn't know. You'd better tell me.'

'I wouldn't know either, but this I know: Fleece would have sat tight till kingdom come. But he didn't, and that's the coincidence. He changed his mind very abruptly. He changed his mind directly after Kincaid turned up at the Asterbury.'

Gently shrugged. 'What makes you think there's a connection?'

'Coincidence. Timing. It's all too pat. That divorce was the biggest shock on earth; it was the last thing that either of us expected. And there has to be a reason for a thing like that. It would need to be something out of the everyday run. Something like a man coming back from the dead, and a lot of publicity: and a lot of questions! It fits too well, there must be a connection. Kincaid returns, and Fleece files his divorce suit.'

'*Post hoc, propter hoc,* as you'd no doubt tell me.'

'It's nothing of the sort. It goes further than that. In some way you don't know about they were mixed up together, and until you find out what it is you'll never understand this case.'

'And you haven't found it out either?'

'No. Also, I'm not blind.'

'Hasn't Mrs Fleece told you?'

'She knows nothing about her husband's secrets.'

'Or you about hers?'

'What are you getting at now?'

'I'm trying to get at what you know about Mrs Paula Kincaid Fleece.'

He didn't take it in immediately, but when he did it was a visible shock. He sank back on the stool with a heavy, clumsy motion. 'That can't – that can't be true. I've known them both. They're different people.'

'About Sarah's build, you said. And both addicted to dyeing their hair.'

'But no . . . I couldn't have met Sarah before!'

'The reason for Fleece's sudden divorce.'

'I know it fits, but it isn't true.'

'The factor that mixed them up together.'

'No!' Heslington shook his head with vigour. 'You've got it wrong. I know you have. Sarah has told me all about her life. Why should she have lied to me about that?'

'She may have her reasons.'

'You don't understand! We're . . . well, we *have* no secrets from each other. And you can check it easily; you don't have to guess. She was married to Fleece at Penwood, near Dorking.'

Gently's nod was ponderous. 'Or we can ask the lady herself. In fact, I think we might as well do that. And perhaps you would like to come along with us.'

'Willingly.' Heslington rose again quickly, and then he paused. 'But unfortunately, it can't be today.'

'Why not?'

'She's in Horsham. She's gone to visit her daughter. You upset her a bit yesterday and she felt she needed cheering up.'

Gently kept on nodding. He felt in his pocket for his pipe.

CHAPTER EIGHT

GENTLY HAD FINISHED. Evans showed an inclina-
tion to linger with Heslington, but when the
Yard man made a move he followed obediently out to
the car. They both stood still in the rain for a moment,
looking back at that remarkable house, which even
more now they were outside it seemed to resemble a
mislaid stage set. Then they got back into the car.

Gently mused: 'That was one for the record! Was he
like that when you saw him before, when you were
questioning him in Wales?'

'Well, he wasn't wearing a toga. They aren't a lot of
use on Snowdon.' Evans answered the question
seriously, as though its technical side was of interest.
'He was much the same apart from that: a little peculiar
in his ways.'

'The stage has lost something there.'

'You think it was all put on, man?'

'Not all of it. But there wasn't much he didn't
underline with greasepaint.'

'So what shall we do about him?'

'Nothing . . . he's given me a touch of Kincaiditis. I want to think about him carefully in case he tempts me to do something rash. But either way we've lost Kincaid, unless something damning turns up. We couldn't prosecute with a principal witness who might have done the job himself.'

'No, man. I'd worked that out. It's either Heslington or nothing. And to my way of thinking we might as well turn Kincaid loose.'

'So you're still backing Heslington.'

'I am, I'm telling you.' Evans eyed him mournfully. His Welsh face was long and sad. 'Don't forget there were only two up there, even if Heslington is telling the truth; and I see it plainly now that we can never swear to the other one. So that leaves us with Heslington, telling a lie with a circumstance, and enough motive in his pockets to sink a Cunard liner. It's a case, man; it's the only case. We'll get nothing else out of it. It rests with those two; and we've practically eliminated Kincaid.'

'I wonder.' Gently brooded over the traffic on the Hill. 'Nothing's impossible with Kincaid. He takes whole Everests in his stride. And the case against Heslington is motive and opportunity to nothing: not a winning combination, from a prosecutor's viewpoint.'

'Do you think we wouldn't get a conviction?'

'I'm sure we wouldn't. It's too doubtful. There's no attacking Heslington's story of his movements on Snowdon. And he'll make a sympathetic figure, his defence will see to that, and Fleece the reverse. No jury would give us a conviction.'

'Then did we ought to drop the case, and save the public some money?'

Gently grinned. 'Not just yet. Not with the results still coming in. And as for turning Kincaid loose, he's much too useful where he is. While the charge is still against him, there's a chance of other people being careless.'

Evans lit a cigarette and jetted smoke at the car's roof.

'There's the Mrs Kincaid angle,' he said. 'That might tie the case a bit tighter. If she's Mrs Fleece, and Heslington knew, and he lured Kincaid to Wales to implicate him, that would show a prior plan and give the jury something to chew at.'

'Mmn.' Gently was tepid. 'It's time we sorted that out, in any case. We'd better apply to Somerset House and stop waiting for Dorking. Only documents can lie. It's easy to give false particulars. What we need are some witnesses who remember Mrs Fleece as Sarah Amies.'

'But there won't be any if she wasn't.'

'That's the hard fact of the matter. And from what Dorking has told us so far, it doesn't seem so wide of the mark.'

He dropped Evans, who seemed keen on the assignment, at Somerset House and returned to his office to make an abortive call to Dorking. The inspector in charge there was deferentially apologetic, but was apparently no nearer to finding the answers to Gently's inquiries.

'It's all sixes and sevens at Penwood. This is only one of the balls-ups. They've just opened a new registry office and the older records are in a mess. As for the Vicar, the old Penwood man, he's staying with his children in America. We sent him a cable this morning and we're expecting to hear from him.'

'What about the Baxters or Blackstables in their house near the church?'

'Well, actually, they're all new houses there now. We've made inquiries at the post office and they remember some people called Ballinger, but they moved during the war and their forwarding address has been destroyed. They were elderly then.'

'Nobody remembers any Amieses?'

'Not so far. Only Amyas, Armes, and Amble . . .'

Kincaid! He hung up and then rang for a cup of coffee. He sat drinking it and smoking while he peered out of the window. Across the courtyard and over the Embankment the yellowish Thames rolled obscurely, and the sculptured cliffs of County Hall winked their multitudinous lights. How many records did it hold, that neighbouring monster over the river? How many were here, in the innumerable filing systems of Scotland Yard? And throughout London and all the country there existed such collections: in such a wilderness of papers, what hope was there of tracing one?

Yet somewhere in some of those files must lie the answer to his riddles. They could settle the issue of Mrs Kincaid, of Fleece's money, and of Stanley's interest. It was a tantalizing thought. Somewhere these facts were in black and white. If he could have magically assembled the documents a map of the affair would be lying in front of him . . .

There would go Kincaid, the younger Kincaid, a callow young man fresh up from the country; taking his very junior appointment in the firm where Fleece was already an executive. How did they meet, this unlikely pair? At work, at play; at a social evening? Sharing a rope on the kindly Tryfan, or exchanging partners at the annual works hop? For meet they did, and became acquainted, if not exactly on visiting terms: the pushing young manager of a small department and the lowly pay-clerk at his furthest desk . . .

Then there was the third, the comptometer operator, making her awkward journey on the Tube each morning: Sloane Square, changing at Charing Cross, Edgware-Morden to Hendon Central. Young; good-looking; not a little ambitious; very probably spoiled by her widowed mother; titivating herself with daring hairdos, and spending the best part of her money on clothes. Naturally, she'd work in or close to the pay department. What was it that attracted her: his strangeness? His provincial oddity? Had the sought-after Paula felt sorry for Kincaid, a mothering fondness for the motherless young fellow . . . ?

A Rolls-Royce slicked into the courtyard, momentarily displacing his train of thought; not the Commissioner's sombre state-waggon, but a gorgeous beast in electric blue. He watched it cynically over his pipe. Another film star who'd lost her pearls? An ash-blonde stepped from it with a swirl of mink, but she was too far away for him to recognize her.

He dismissed her with a grunt and went back to his musings: Kincaid, Paula, and her unexpected choice. Passing over Arthur Fleece – surely he'd met her at that time? – and all the more obvious and probable candidates. Did she know what she was taking on, in that vanished church in pre-war London? Had she intended to buckle-to as the wife of a wage-earning nobody? She'd perhaps continue with her job at Metropolitan Electric, since that house in Putney must have swallowed a lot of cash; and the gilt would wear off, the hectic romance fall flat, the feeling grow that she'd been a fool and thrown away her chances . . .

And Fleece was there to remind her of one of the chances she'd thrown away; seeing her now in a new light, as the jewel another man had snatched up. A beauty undeservedly annexed, and a discontented beauty; ready to think again and this time to grasp with a better reach. And Fleece could see fortune. He'd discovered the ways and means. He'd got a tourniquet in his hand and was ready to try his luck with a squeeze. For a man like him, wasn't she the woman: fair, sophisticated, a social asset; good enough and ambitious enough, but not expensive: the very thing?

Gently paused to backtrack on that. Was he quite sure it was sound? Wasn't there something slightly amiss with that part of the picture? An ambitious man might have looked higher, above the level of Kincaid's wife; a climber himself, he would want a mate who was already to some extent in possession. That was the flaw in the fabric; a blind passion was out of the question; he was too much in Fleece's skin to believe that love had been the moving force. It might have piqued his pride to obtain her and he might have considered her had she been single, but as it was had the prize been worth the effort, including Everest and attempted murder? Obviously not, to a man like Fleece, a chilly egoist and a weigher of chances. It was an insufficient motive, the motive was much more likely to have been money. And he had returned, having disposed of Kincaid, to collect what must have been a substantial sum, paid by someone, it had to follow, to whom Kincaid had spelled danger. Yet who could Kincaid have threatened, that obscure little pay-clerk? What terrible secret had he learned and perhaps still carried in his head?

It seemed improbable; but if it were true, till now Gently had been pursuing a chimera, and the disappearance of Mrs Kincaid took on a darker, more sinister aspect . . .

His phone buzzed; he grabbed it impatiently. It was the sergeant on the desk.

'There's a lady here wants to see you, sir. Gives the name of Mrs Askham.'

'Tell her I'm busy.'

'It's about your case, sir. She wants you and nobody else.'

'What about my case?'

'She won't say, sir. A bit upstage, the lady is.'

Gently hesitated. 'She isn't that blonde, is she? The one who drove up in a Rolls?'

'. . . wearing mink, sir. That's the one.'

Gently fingered his tie. 'Very well. Send her up.'

131

He shrugged largely, shaking his head: out of the blue it was coming, this one! The name of Askham rang no bells, nothing in society or on the stage or screen. He was belatedly reaching for his copy of *Who's Who* when his door was tapped and the lady walked in.

'I read in the papers that you were anxious to trace Kincaid's wife, Superintendent. Since I was in London I thought I would call on you. Paula Kincaid used to be my secretary.'

She was superb. She was in the manner of women who have always had the bank behind them. She sat with legs meticulously crossed and her chin held at a patrician angle. Beneath her mink she wore a lilac suit, and it matched exactly the tint of her eyes; the legs, whole worlds from being mere limbs, were barely sheened with nylon mist. Perhaps the last thing one noticed about her, if one succeeded in noticing it at all, was that her age was 'twenty-nine', it might be almost approaching thirty. She spoke with a ringingly modulated voice which was also distinct from the purely functional.

'You are still interested in the woman, are you?'

'Oh yes!' Gently assembled his truant wits.

'Because if you aren't I won't continue to waste my time and yours. As it is, my information is probably of doubtful value. But I had an hour between engagements and I thought that this might fill it in.'

'You are very kind, Mrs Askham.'

She flicked him a look from between well-brushed lashes. Some delicate shadowing, a touch of crimson, they were eyes a camera would have doted on, and at the distance of a desk the effect was quite breath-taking. Her angelic hair was swept up in a high wave and caught in a web of lilac organdie.

'First, you'd like to have my particulars. I am Mrs Harry Askham. My town address is in Mount Street; I left my card down at the desk. My late husband, as no doubt you know, was what is called an industrial magnate. He was a cousin of Lord Cliffley's and related to the Blount family.'

She paused, as though intending to let these particulars sink in. Then she said:

'I think it likely that Mrs Kincaid is still in Wales. My country place is at Beaumaris, and we were living there when I discharged her. She was fond of Wales, as she often told me, and I heard later that she was living at Caernarvon.'

Gently rocked a little in his chair. This was too much, coming all in one mouthful! After so much painful and laboured digging, now to have it handed to him on a platter . . . ! How many people were there around like this, waiting for an hour between their engagements, or just not bothering at all, not giving a damn for the oafish police?

He became aware of Mrs Askham watching him suspiciously.

'I wouldn't be boring you, would I?' she asked.

'No. Far from it.'

'I only ask because I don't want you to think me a pest. You must get a number of frivolous callers who imagine they have important information, and I should hate to be classed as one of them. This is my first visit to the police.'

'I assure you I'm very interested.'

'Then would you like to ask me some questions?'

'I would. I would indeed.'

Mrs Askham complacently smoothed her skirt.

'When did you engage Paula Kincaid, Mrs Askham?'

'When? Oh, in the summer of nineteen-thirty-seven. She was a widow, you know, or thought she was. Rather teary and mournful. Though she soon got over it.'

'Did you engage her through an agency?'

'Oh no. My husband suggested her.'

'Your husband?'

'Harry Askham. He knew I was looking for a secretary. When you're running three establishments and that sort of thing, then a secretary becomes essential. Otherwise you'd go mad.'

'But how did your husband come to know of her?'

'He employed her, of course; she worked at the firm. He thought it would be doing the girl a good turn, or so he said at the time.'

'And his firm?' Gently gaped.

Her lilac eyes opened reprovingly.

'Metropolitan Electric. Harry *was* Met. L.'

Did she know she was a bombshell, sitting there so expensively, with a hint of the air of a duchess extracting amusement from a clown? If she did, she didn't show it. She'd learned not to wrinkle her precious skin. And her eyes, cool and bold, merely stared at him interestedly.

'You mean . . . before the merger?' Gently grasped for the phrase blindly.

'Oh yes. And afterwards too. It was we who took over Intrics, you know. Harry continued as managing director up to his death nine years ago; then Clarence Stanley was appointed, chiefly at my instigation. I was never actually on the Board, though of course I own the controlling interest.'

'Then Mr Stanley is . . . well known to you?'

'Naturally. I wanted a man I could trust.'

'He would follow your instructions?'

'He would consult me on matters of policy.'

Her eyes twinkled and she added: 'He hadn't consulted me about yesterday. But he knew the girl had been my secretary, and he was doing his loyal best to protect me. Clarence has always been a dear.'

'Hmn.' Gently didn't sound so certain of it. 'And that's the reason for your visit today? Because Mr Stanley was unsuccessful?'

She regarded him archly. 'That's not a kind way to put it, but it's close to the truth, so I'll forgive you. Also I thought if I saw you myself I might persuade you to spare me publicity. I dread an appearance in the popular press. I prefer the greater sympathy of the *Illustrated*.'

Gently shrugged. 'I can give you no promises.'

'You'll do your best. I feel confident of that.'

'If I can lay hands on Paula Kincaid I won't be ungrateful. That's the most I can offer.'

She nodded. She picked up her sharkskin bag, which she'd laid on the desk with her pair of lilac gloves. She

135

produced a slender silver case and a butane lighter, both flowingly monogrammed and engraved with a crest.

'May I offer you a cigarette?'

Gently accepted from curiosity. But they were honest-to-goodness Player's and not the gold-tipped confection he'd expected. She held out the lighter with a long-fingered hand, the nails of which were polished only. She held it steadily. Her only ring was a circle of gold on the third finger.

'Now that we've examined my motives, shall we continue with Paula Kincaid?'

'If we may.' The unaccustomed cigarette smoke was making Gently squint.

'I engaged her after Ascot, it must have been the end of June, and in July she accompanied us to Trecastles, at Beaumaris. Trecastles is Harry's family place. We were both very fond of it; it looks across the Straits to Llanfairfechan, with the Great Orme in the distance. Paula wasn't a secretary, of course, she'd worked an adding machine or something, but she was an adaptable sort of girl and soon picked up the job. She was rather flighty, I'm afraid to say. She was always doing things with her hair.' Mrs Askham inhaled delicately and allowed herself the luxury of a frown.

'She found a boyfriend, did she?'

The frown lingered. 'I'm coming to that. I may be doing her less than justice, but I made up my mind I would confide in you. That was the summer I was having Henry, who is our only child, so I couldn't keep an eye on things as much as I'd have liked. Harry kept a yacht down there, and I didn't always feel like

136

sailing. Then there were excursions I was sometimes out of. Having a baby is no joke. Am I making myself plain?'

'Reasonably plain, Mrs Askham.'

'I'm glad, because I shall never know the truth of it myself. Harry was a man and inclined that way, he would have been unhealthy if he wasn't; but there are limits, you'll agree. I drew a line at the servants.'

'Did you tackle him about it?'

'No. Not beyond hinting. There was never sufficient to go on, not till the day I sacked her.'

'When was that?'

'It was during the war, it would be in nineteen-forty-one. I caught him kissing her in the shelter during an alert. And out she went.'

'What was your husband's reaction to that?'

'What could it be? He simply saw nothing. Harry was a husband of the greatest tact. It was a quality I always appreciated in him.'

'Do you know if he saw her again after she left?'

'He may have done, since she certainly remained in the district. My housekeeper at Trecastles ran across her in Caernarvon perhaps a year after that. But she no longer concerned me.'

'And that was positively the last you've heard of her?'

'Yes, positively. When Davies saw her.'

'Did she tell your housekeeper what she was doing?'

'No. Davies received the impression that she wasn't in employment.'

Gently drew at the cigarette, which his clumsy

fingers were making squashy. Surely *l'affaire* Kincaid couldn't be reduced to these proportions? The passing whim of a millionaire for the wife of one of his obscure employees, involving murder by proxy and the disbursement of two large sums? It was top-heavy; it was taking a steam-hammer to crack the shell of a nut. Askham's purpose could have been served at a far lesser rate. It looked more as though he'd accepted an opportunity already made, adding to his household a likely recruit whom he could seduce at his leisure. Unless . . . unless his motive was something other than it seemed: such as the deliberate seclusion of Mrs Kincaid and the severing of her ties with her past. But why? What did she know? From whom was her information to be kept? From the returning members of the expedition; from the designing Fleece; could that have been it? He ground the cigarette into his tray.

'Where did Paula Kincaid spend most of her time?'

Mrs Askham's eyes looked wondering. 'With us, of course. Wherever we were.'

'In Wales for the most part?'

'For the most part in Wales. We always looked on Trecastles as being our home. And that first year, having Henry, I didn't bother about the season.'

'So she was in Wales during all her first year with you?'

'Except at Christmas, when we went to a party at Cannes. Then the next summer we went to Scotland: Harry wanted to cruise the Western Isles; and after the shooting we returned to Wales, and after that on to

Cannes. Then I suppose it was Wales again. It was dull in town; too many war scares.'

'But you'd go to town to do your shopping. To see your dressmaker and the like?'

Mrs Askham said very coldly: 'I buy my clothes from Balmain.'

'So in fact Paula Kincaid was rarely in London?'

'I suppose she wasn't. But she didn't complain.'

'Did she ever go there to visit her mother?'

'Her mother was dead, I seem to remember.'

'Where did she spend her holidays?'

Mrs Askham was vague. 'I let her off when we were abroad, she usually preferred it that way. Then after the war started we spent most of the time at Trecastles, and she never seemed to want a holiday. But perhaps that was Harry's doing.'

'How do you mean?' Gently asked sharply.

Her eyes wondered at him again. 'I should have thought that was obvious. He was always keen to keep her near him.'

It fitted perfectly. He had spirited her away from all her pre-expedition contacts, had carried her off to his castle in Wales and had held her there incommunicado. By contrivance or a hefty bribe, he had secured her consent to this: and it was only an ill-timed kiss in a shelter that had brought the arrangement to an end. How had it been managed after that? Davies, the housekeeper, suggested the answer. He had set up house for Paula in Caernarvon and had perhaps endowed her with an annuity. And now, eighteen years later, Fleece had shown cognizance of this development. His mysterious trips into Wales now throbbed with a blatant significance. But why had Fleece waited to use his knowledge until the re-appearance of Kincaid? What subtle condition had been fulfilled, and who had it driven to take drastic action? Not Askham, he was dead; blackmail couldn't reach him any longer. But there was Stanley, the father-figure, who might have inherited the Met. L secrets . . .

'You said you had little to do with your husband's business affairs, Mrs Askham.'

'That's perfectly true, if it helps you. Though I'm not entirely a fool in business.'

'You place great faith in Mr Stanley?'

'Mr Stanley is my best friend. He and Harry were at Oxford together and they were more like brothers than most brothers I know.'

Gently's tone was deferential. 'This may seem irrelevant, but it could have a bearing on the subject of my inquiries. Did your husband have any business anxieties?'

'It certainly does seem irrelevant.' Mrs Askham let it hang for a moment, her eyes half interrogative, half scornful. 'However, I suppose you have a reason for asking, and I came here to be helpful, so I'll answer the question. Yes, he did appear anxious about something.'

'To do with the business?'

'I presumed so. I wasn't entirely in Harry's confi-dence. But in latter years he seemed rather harassed, and that I believe had an effect on his health. But whatever it was could not have been serious, since the firm has suffered no setbacks. I checked particularly about it with Clarence. He could think of nothing that should have worried Harry.'

'Your husband knew Arthur Fleece, I'm told.'

'Did he? He knew all sorts of people.'

'Can you remember any visits Fleece made him?'

'No. I'm sorry. I have a bad memory for faces.'

Gently opened a drawer and took from it the photograph he'd obtained from Mrs Fleece. He pushed it across the desk, watching Mrs Askham intently.

'Did this man ever visit your husband?'

Her eyes flickered. 'No. I'm sure of it.'

'It isn't a face that's easily forgotten.'

'I warned you. My memory for faces is bad.'

'Then why are you sure he didn't visit your husband?'

'I . . . oh well, perhaps I was being too positive. But I don't remember him, I can assure you of that. And you're right about the face. It really gives one the shivers.'

She smiled dismissingly and rose to her feet, retrieving the sharkskin bag and the gloves; the duchess who'd more than done her duty and who now intended to seek other diversions.

'I'm afraid I shall have to be getting along. I have an appointment to keep at André's. I'm reposing in you the strictest confidence, Superintendent: not a whisper of our little chat to the Press.'

He nodded vaguely. 'Thank you for coming, Mrs Askham.' He rose and accompanied her to the door.

'I've enjoyed it thoroughly and you've been very

kind. I shall tell Clarence he's quite mistaken in his views about our police force.'

When she'd gone, when the door was closed, Gently stood for a few moments thinking; then he chuckled and went to the window to watch the blue Rolls drive away in the rain.

CHAPTER NINE

IT WAS HALF an hour later when Evans returned, and Gently was sprawled at his desk again, nursing another cup of coffee. The Welshman began sniffing as soon as he stepped into the room, and after a sharp look round he glanced suspiciously at Gently.

'That's not Gold Block, man, I do know,' he said.

'Chanel.' Gently pretended to leer. 'There's still some glamour left in being in homicide.'

'You're telling me, man. And I only let you out of my sight for five minutes. Tell me, what would be my chances of getting a transfer to the Central Office?'

Gently waved an airy hand. 'It needs personality,' he replied. 'But I'll give you the scandal in a minute. Tell me the news from Somerset House.'

Evans dropped down on the chair which had lately been occupied by Mrs Askham.

'There isn't any, man,' he said. 'News disgusts them over at that place.'

'It'll require a day or two, will it?'

'You take the words out of their mouth. Nearly

laughed at me they did when I told them I'd be waiting. I see now why you went to Dorking. The long way round is down the Strand. We'll be lucky to hear from them by next year's Eisteddfod,'

'They handle a deal of business, of course.' Gently sipped at his coffee. 'But as it happens it doesn't matter. I've a feeling that trail can be written off.'

'You're on a new scent. I can smell that.'

'It's just a whiff that came in from the bank. But it brought some other smells along with it and I'm still trying to sort them out.'

He outlined his interview with Mrs Askham, and Evans listened to him in silence; but it wasn't difficult to read the expression that slowly developed on the inspector's face. Here was ground for fresh hope. Kincaid had not eluded them yet. The excitement grew in Evans's eyes, and at the end he exclaimed:

'Then we're back, man. We're back where we started. It's just the way I had in mind. Kincaid did see his wife in Caernarvon — and as a result of it, he murdered Fleece!'

'On the facts it's possible.' Gently sounded discouraging.

'But goodness, you can't miss it, it fits them like an old shoe. Fleece had been at her, he was going to marry her; that was the reason for his divorce. Then away comes Kincaid and learns about it, and the rest just follows on natural.'

'But why should Fleece want to marry Paula Kincaid?'

'Because she knows something. That's what it will be. She knows something that didn't matter as long as

Kincaid was dead, but when he came back Fleece had to marry her to be safe from her evidence.'

It was a good point; Gently considered it.

'But what could it be that she knew?'

'Something to do with what happened on Everest.' Evans gave him a sapient nod. 'You think a moment. There's no harm in supposing that Paula Kincaid was once his mistress. We keep looking at it from Fleece's angle and there's no call for that at all. It may have been her who wanted Kincaid away. It may have been her who persuaded Fleece to do it. Then, when it was done, she pulls up her stakes and disappears; to avoid answering awkward questions and perhaps giving herself away. Wouldn't that be a good reason for her taking a job with Mrs Askham? And for staying in Wales too, after Mrs Askham sacked her?'

'Then why was she worrying Fleece?'

'Do you ask, man, with Kincaid back? He was spreading an awfully suspicious story, and scouring the country for his wife. Perhaps Fleece wasn't worried at first, not till he'd talked to Paula Kincaid; and perhaps it was her who was doing the worrying; perhaps it was she who suggested the divorce. It would be unnatural if Kincaid had not suspected his wife, but once she'd married Fleece, well then they'd be fireproof.'

'It fits,' Gently conceded.

It does. It must do.' Evans's red face split in a triumphant grin. 'By the beard of Cadwalader, I'll be a superintendent yet, and boss my own show back there in Caernarvon. Now we've only to find Paula Kincaid.'

'In Caernarvon or out of it.'

Evans' face sank. 'Do you think she'll have hopped it?' he asked.

'Do you ask, man?' Gently mimicked. 'She'd be out of there like a scalded cat. You might look for her at John o' Groats, but you'll scarcely find her in Caernarvon.'

'That's true enough.' Evans was dour again. 'There had to be a catch in it somewhere. And we must lay our hands on her if we're to make it stick to Kincaid. But you must admit, man, we're seeing our way, we've got the drift of it now. It's only a question of time and routine before we sew up the case.'

'Have you forgotten our friend, Heslington?'

'Oh, to hell with that fellow.'

'And a few other matters, like two large sums of money?'

Evans made a rude noise. 'So what is that to us now? A couple of years in Somerset House and you'll perhaps find where Fleece got his money. And as for the other – well, what about it? So there were philanthropists before the war. If we studied every little coincidence we'd never have a case at all, man.'

As though in comment on this bold line Gently's telephone buzzed, and after an intervention from the board he found himself connected to Overton.

'I looked up that address you wanted, the solicitors who signed the banker's order. They're Sedley and Haines in Lincoln's Inn . . . Yes, I've got their number here.'

Gently jotted it down, thanked Overton and gave

the number to the board. Evans, his thumbs under his lapels, awaited the issue with elaborate insouciance.

'Sedley and Haines? This is Superintendent Gently of Scotland Yard . . . I'd like to speak to one of the partners. It's about a commission you had before the war.'

To Evans it seemed to take an hour before the suspicious lawyers would come to business. Twice Gently repeated himself and he gave numerous though vague assurances. At last the receiver was returned to its rest. Evans rocked gently back in his chair.

'Who was it then? Nuffield or William Lever?'

Gently's hazel eyes twinkled. 'It was your coincidence,' he said.

'But does it make so much difference when all's said and done?'

Evans was still arguing the point though his mouth was full of buttered crumpet. Sitting at a table in the canteen, a buttery knife in his hand, he ate steadily and drank many cups as he tried to win Gently to his way of thinking.

'Look at it straight, now. Who would you have expected to donate that money? Why, Askham; weren't two of his employees in the expedition? And Fleece, he was one of the management, Askham may have spoken to him about it, and you remember how Overton told us that Fleece had suddenly changed his attitude. What could be more natural, then? Why does it need to be sinister? Askham was interested, he admired their spirit, so he came across with the necessary.'

Gently deftly severed a crumpet; he was looking his woodenest and most obstinate.

'He came across with ten thousand pounds?'

'But that was chicken feed to the fellow!'

'And anonymously.'

'Why not? Some rich men are like that.'

'With Met. L to advertise?'

'He was modest, that's all.'

'He went yachting and shooting, but I didn't hear he was a climbing enthusiast.'

'Oh St David listen to him!' Evans bolted a savage crumpet. He seized his cup and irrigated the morsel with a number of full-throated gulps. 'Then what do we do? Where do we go? What's the next step from here? Either we chase up Paula Kincaid or we stick the case in the files!'

Gently sipped more abstemiously. 'Things aren't quite so desperate,' he returned.

'We've got Kincaid in a vice if we can only turn up his missus!'

'She mightn't talk if we did. Also, we don't know where to look for her. And in the meantime it was Askham who footed the bill for the expedition.'

Evans snatched up another crumpet and began unconsciously to chew it. He felt a pang of pity for the Assistant Commissioner, who had to deal with Gently day by day. 'Very well, man,' he said. 'I wash my hands of it from now on. I've said my say, and I stand by it. And now I should like to hear your views.'

Gently's hand gestured indefinitely. 'Mine are still unsettled, I'm afraid. I'm still groping in the dark for what happened in nineteen-thirty-seven. There's a reason behind that ten thousand pounds, but for the moment I can't see the shape of it . . . Kincaid knew something, but what did he know? Was it he who was trying to blackmail Askham?'

'You'll scarcely find that out now,' retorted Evans with satisfaction. 'And if it's blackmail you have in mind I'll stick to Fleece for a client.'

'It would have to be something ruinous. Perhaps affecting Met. L. And his wife would have to know something too, because in an involuntary way, she was also dangerous; and Askham was keeping her under wraps, that's fairly certain from the evidence. But from whom, with Kincaid dead and Fleece apparently in the secret? If a member of the expedition were aimed at, how could his curiosity be threatening? If it wasn't his wife behind Kincaid's disappearance, she could be left in ignorance to play the widow, but if she was privy to it, as you suppose, then why is Askham so deeply in the plot? We're left with the unlikely supposition that Askham and she had separate motives, that they were equally responsible, and together contrived her own disappearance. And that' – Gently gave Evans an amiable smile – 'sounds like a lot of moonshine to me. It meets the facts in a sort of way, but it collides head-on with common sense.'

'So?' Evans was far from placated.

'So the facts are wrong. Or we've missed their significance.'

'If you'll just let that money be a coincidence . . .'

'It's a coincidence too often, which means that it isn't one.'

Gently drank. His eye drifted away from Evans, seemed to vanish through the murals on the wall behind him; it was uncanny, it made Evans feel uncomfortable, it was as though the Yard man had disembodied himself. Evans made a clatter with his knife and plate to interrupt the phenomenon.

'In reality it will be much simpler . . .' Gently returned from his distant oracle. 'There'll be a pattern that a child can understand; it isn't the way of murder to be complex. We're making heavy weather of something. I can't put a finger on it yet. But it's got its roots in what happened before the war, and when we make a breakthrough there . . .'

'But how do you propose doing that, man?' Evans refused to lose sight of the practical. 'We've covered all the leads we've got, and it's unlikely we'll turn up anything fresh.'

'I think Mrs Askham did remember Fleece.'

'She'd never let on. She'd be a fool if she did.'

'There's also Stanley. If we could put pressure on him . . .'

'Isn't it more likely that he'll put pressure on us, man?'

'And there's Paula Kincaid.'

'Now you're talking, man.' Evans brightened visibly; this was where he'd come in. 'We can go to Caernarvon and try to pick up her trail. I'll phone Williams at once. I'm sure we'll get on to her.'

'She may have married or changed her name.'

'It won't make so much difference—' Evans broke off to scowl at a police cadet who had approached their table. The youngster came to attention, giving his heels a click.

'Superintendent Gently, sir. A message from the desk.'

'What is it?'

'There's a lady wants to speak to you, sir.'

Evans gazed at the lad. 'Not another one. Why, there's no holding the fellow!'

Gently asked: 'What's her name?'

'Sir. A Miss Paula Kincaid.'

'Paula Kincaid I am, and I live up in Kilburn. I'm an artist's model, and I'll thank you to remember it.'

If Gently's disappointment was keen, he was at pains to keep it hidden; he sat unmoved behind his desk, eyeing his new conquest with mild gravity.

'Haven't I seen you before?'

'Well, p'raps you have and p'raps you haven't. This is my first time down this way, but I've had the treatment back in Kilburn.'

'Under the name of Paula Kincaid?'

'Don't be daft! That's me proper name. I'm Phyllis Waters on the charge sheet. It makes a change from Smif and Brown.'

She was barely twenty, but she carried herself with a hard self-possession. She was a little above the average in height, a peroxide blonde with brown, unashamed eyes. She had on a bushy-skirted gown of green and over it a short coat of fabricated fur, her stockings were black and her shoes had stub-heels and apart from her mouth she wasn't heavily made up.

151

'Have you brought your birth certificate with you?'

'Go on. I haven't got one of them things. Got lost, that would've done, years ago. And I don't know where I was born, so I can't get another one.'

'What's your age?'

'Eighteen I am. I had me birthday last month.'

'So why have you come to see me, Paula?'

'About me ma, of course. Reg Kincaid's missus.'

Self-possession; she had that, but it was the stock-in-trade of a street-girl. Unless you had it you didn't take to the business in the first place. You had to tell a lie with a lot of clamour and always have an act ready for the police; you were tough: brazen they used to call it: you put on a burlesque all the time. She sat confidently with her feet apart, her shoes turned over, the stub-heels outwards. She'd be capable of staring down the devil if Gently by chance should adopt the role.

'Why did you decide to do that? Because you usually assist the police?'

'Naow – don't talk silly!' Her beaming smile wasn't entirely false. 'But it won't do me no harm, that's the way I looks at it, and it could do me a bit of good. So here I am.'

'You won't get any money.'

'Didn't ask for none, did I? But you could pass the word I come to see you; had been of assistance, you could say that.'

'And that was your whole motive in coming?'

'Ain't it good enough for you? Coo, I reckon it's a bit of jam, me coming in here like this.'

He couldn't help it, he returned the smile. She had

152

a streak of Cockney charm about her. A graceless, graceful, perky sparrowness, the quick gaiety of the London pavements.

'All right,' he said. 'You're Paula Kincaid. You've come to tell me something about your ma. And the first thing you can tell me is where your ma is at this moment.'

'That's the point, dear. She ain't anywhere. Least-ways, not above ground.'

'You mean she's dead?'

'And buried, she is. She was killed in the blitz in forty-three.'

'*Where was she buried?*'

'Now do me a favour! I was only two when they buried me ma.'

'But you must know where it was.'

'I'm telling you, ain't I? I never went to the funeral. Don't even know if they dug up enough of her to bury. A blockbuster it was. Over Notting Hill way.'

Gently gave her the benefit of a long, pointed look. There was something too Kincaid-like about this unsolicited tale! It promised to end things so neatly, so finally, so irrefutably; drawing a firm straight line across all further investigation . . .

'Who told you what happened to your mother?'

'Gertie Fox, what brought me up. Ma had took me to Gertie's on the night when it happened.'

'Why did your mother do that?'

''Cause she was on the bash, she was. And so was Gertie, if you want to know, but she used to have me there all the same.'

153

'And where does this Gertie live?'

'She had a flat down Maida once. But then she married the bloke what was looking after her. I ain't seen Gertie since she did that.'

'So in effect you can't substantiate any of these statements?'

'Didn't say I could, did I? It's take it or leave it.'

'Who put you up to coming here?'

'Not nobody didn't. I come here on me own.'

She smiled again; but Gently had finished with smiling. He picked up a pencil and did some scribbling on a pad. He passed the result to Evans, who read it frowningly and then nodded. He rose and left the office. Their visitor's eyes followed him uneasily.

'Where's *he* gorn off to?'

Gently's answer was merely to stare. He filled his pipe unhurriedly and spent a couple of matches lighting it.

Now,' he said. 'Let's hear all you know about your mother, Miss Kincaid. And about your father, too. I dare say Gertie will have mentioned him.'

She was seeming far less happy, but she had a good shot at it. Gertie indeed had filled her in on a number of interesting points. She knew that her 'ma' had come from Wales and had 'done all right for herself' there, but that she'd mucked it up somehow and on her return to London had become a prostitute. When that return had been, Miss Kincaid wasn't certain, nor whether she'd been born in Wales or in London. As for her father, she had the impression that he'd been her mother's employer in Wales.

'What was his name?'

'I didn't never know. Ma kept quiet about that for some reason. But he was a bloke with a lot of money. A millionaire, Gertie reckoned he was.'

'Didn't he pay your mother an allowance?'

'Well, he might have done, for all I know. But it never stopped her from going on the bash, so it couldn't have been much if he did, could it?'

'How did you learn who her husband had been?'

'It came up one day through something in the paper. Gertie says to me, "Look. Here's a picture of your ma's old man." It was in one of them Sunday papers, a bit about some people climbing Everest.'

'And you got in touch with him when you heard he was alive?'

'Naow! Why should I? Nothink to me, he wasn't.'

'He was trying to find his wife. You could have told him what happened to her.'

'So what? I'm one of those what keeps meself to meself.'

'Tell me about yourself from the time you were left with Gertie.'

She'd been with Gertie until she was sixteen. She said that distinctly, pausing after it. Before then she'd been to school, 'just one of them schools down in Maida.' At the age of fifteen she'd gone to work in an office, the address of which she succeeded in giving, but the boss was for ever making passes at her so she thought she'd better leave. Then she'd got tangled up with a boyfriend – after her sixteenth birthday, of course – and she'd gone to live with him in Kilburn, where he rented a flat in Crossgrove Road. Here she'd become an 'artist's model', the career which she was now complacently following.

'Does it pay you?' Gently asked cynically.

'I'm not one as talks about me private affairs. But I will say this, I'm not a pauper, nor I'm never short of a quid. Which is more than you can say for some women with their la-di-da airs.'

So there it was, take it or leave it; and, strangely enough, it carried a wistful conviction. It didn't conflict with what he'd learned from Mrs Askham except in the matter of Davies, her housekeeper. Davies must have noticed that Paula Kincaid was pregnant, though it didn't follow automatically that she would tell her mistress. But for the rest the account tallied, it offered a logical development; without betraying a suspicious knowledge it succeeded in being quite credible.

Or did it deal just a shade hardly with the character of Mrs Kincaid: was it acceptable that she should make the swift descent from social secretary to prostitute? Possibly there . . . possibly not. She'd been going downhill with Askham.

'Have you any trinkets of your mother's. Any jewellery, photographs?'

'She was blitzed, I keep telling you. I ain't got nothing at all.'

'What name do you go under with your friends?'

She stared hard for a second. 'Paula, of course. And sometimes Phyllis . . . it really depends on who I'm with.'

'Why Phyllis?'

'I told you. It's a name I calls meself.'

'Why do you call yourself that to friends?'

'I don't much. Just sometimes.'

'What name does your landlord know you by?'

'Well . . . Phyllis, I'm Phyllis to him.'

'Yet that's the name you've been convicted under?'

'Aow, I don't know! I just use it . . .'

Gently nodded with profundity and struck a fresh light for his pipe. Evans re-entered; from behind Miss Kincaid's back he gave Gently a broad wink. Gently puffed.

'Very well, Miss Kincaid. It was kind of you to call in. Now if you'll leave your name and address I don't think we'll need to detain you.'

'You mean I can go now?' She looked both relieved and surprised. 'It's all right, ain't it?'

'Quite all right. And you can depend on the credit you deserve.'

Her smile was doubtful, but she flashed one. She hastily gave the required particulars. Evans, sauntering over to the window, was quietly whistling 'Men of Harlech'.

'Now can I go?'

'Now you can go.'

'It seemed half as though she didn't want to. But at last she made up her mind and rose, and minced bobbingly over to the door. Evans came across and lowered himself on to the desk. He tapped a cigarette. He tilted his head as he lit it.

'And what do we know now, man?'

Gently stretched himself, eased backwards. 'Quite a lot, man. And I think we'll know a lot more before long.'

'You're not mourning Mrs Kincaid?'

'It was a terrible business, that blitz was.'

'You're telling me. I'm glad we never had such a thing in Caernarvon.'

They smoked; Gently his pipe, Evans a couple of cigarettes. Twenty minutes ticked by in pleasurable meditation. County Hall looked a mansion of stars against the darkening, sullen sky, and the Thames observed its tides invisibly except for occasional wavering flashes. Then the phone rang.

'Dutt reporting, sir. I've got chummie under surveillance. He's sitting in a café in Villiers Street. He's just ordering a pot of tea.'

'Where did you pick him up, Dutt?'

'By the RAF Memorial, sir. He was sitting there in a parked car, a red M.G., of which I've taken the number. She went straight up to it and got in with him.'

'Did you see what happened?'

'Yessir. He gave her some notes. Then he drove to Villiers Street and parked, and she walked off while he went into the café. I'm watching him now: I'm in the box across the street.'

'Who is he, Dutt?'

'Don't know, sir. Nobody we've had dealings with. He's young and fair-ish, around five foot nine, slim build, good looks, wearing a mid-grey lounge suit and a red tie. Prosperous-looking, I'd say, sir.'

Gently nodded to himself. 'Well, pull him in, Dutt. Right away. You can tell him he's wanted for questioning.'

'And if he gives any trouble, sir?'

'Charge him with conspiring to obstruct the police. And Dutt—'

'Yessir?'

'Don't lose him. He's worth his weight in Welsh griffins.'

CHAPTER TEN

SLIM BUILD, GOOD looks, and wearing a mid-grey lounge suit. Dutt, with a flair for the dramatic entrance, had brought his man straight up. And he was an angry young man; his aspect was far from being guilty. He strode threateningly into the room with green eyes seeking whom they could devour. He settled for Gently.

'I'd like to know the meaning of this – this illegal act of detention. I'm going to make such a stink that there'll be a public inquiry!'

'Sit down, Mr . . . who is it?'

'I'm not going to sit down. I want an explanation, this instant, of why I've been seized and dragged in here!'

He smote the desk with his fist. He was an exceedingly angry young man. His age was one- or two-and-twenty and he had a faint moustache on his lip. His hair was very light brown with a side parting and a droop, his skull was round, his ears small, his nose round-tipped, his lips full. He had a determined cleft chin and his slim build was athletic. Though so angry, his voice retained elements of a public-school drawl.

'Don't think you'll get away with it. You've picked on the wrong person for that. I'm not a nobody, I can tell you. I can make people of your sort jump through hoops.'

'Then would you mind confounding us with your name?'

'You see? You don't even know it! You arrest somebody in a public place without even knowing their name. Just let me use that phone for a second.'

'You'll be allowed to use it if we detain you.'

'I'll use it now. I want my solicitor. And just you try to detain Henry Askham.'

Gently's brows lifted. 'Is that your name? Henry Askham?'

'Henry Askham. Who did you think I was – some Cockney wide-boy of your acquaintance? I tell you now—'

'Mrs Askham's son?'

'Yes. Yes! How many more times?'

'You will kindly sit down, Mr Askham.'

'Only after I've used this phone!'

He made a grab for it, but Dutt was there first; he quietly pinioned the young man's arms. Askham struggled viciously and lashed out with his heels, but he was merely a child in the grip of the sergeant.

'If you don't take your hands off, I'll charge you with assault!'

Gently motioned with his head and Dutt forcibly seated his charge. Then after a warning pause he released him and stepped back from the chair. Askham glared whole armouries at Gently, but he didn't attempt to rise again.

'Now, Mr Askham. We've some questions to ask you.'

'And I've some to ask you. I'll need your name for a start.'

'Relating to a certain Phyllis Waters, alias Paula Kincaid.'

'Mine relate to the statement I'm going to give to the Press!'

He was in no way abashed. His ferocious expression continued; like a slender, enraged terrier, he sat quiveringly on the edge of the chair. It passed through Gently's mind that Mrs Askham's life wasn't all honey, though presumably some of the blame must rest with herself. As a mother, she'd perhaps leave a few things to be desired . . .

'What can you tell us about this person?'

'What do you think?' He was nearly shouting. 'She's a prostitute. She lives in Kilburn. She told you herself. I sent her here.'

'Why did you send her, Mr Askham?'

'Oh, my God, must you be so stupid? Because she knew. She knew what happened. She knew that Paula Kincaid was dead.'

'Why did you want her to tell us that?'

'Is it possible to be so dense? To stop your beastly rotten prying and upsetting of my mother. She's being terrorized by your snooping, and I was determined to put a stop to it.'

'You know she came here this afternoon?'

'Of course I do. You drove her to it.'

'She didn't seem so terrified then.'

'Did you think she'd let you see it?'

'But why should she be so anxious, anyway? It was scarcely a crime to employ Paula Kincaid.'

'She was my father's mistress. Don't you understand that? And Mother hides it, but it hurts her as much as ever . . .'

He flushed curiously. He seemed suddenly embarrassed by what he had said. His eyes kept feverishly boring at Gently, the angrier for the crimson in the cheeks under them.

'And I didn't want her to know the rest. I didn't want her to be mixed up in it. That's why I made that girl go to you, so you'd know the truth without us being mixed up in it. I had to pay her; she didn't want to go. I shelled out fifty quid for your benefit . . .'

'So we'd know the truth.'

'Yes, the God's rotten truth! What happened in the end to Father's dear Paula. While you thought she was alive you'd have kept on and on at Mother, but I knew she was dead, and I intended to let you know it. And this is all the thanks I get for it. To be treated like a criminal!'

'*How* did you know the woman was dead?'

Gently was leaning back in his chair, his eyes half closed, but never wandering from the pair that thrust at him so persistently. Askham had wavered; but only for a second. Now his reply came strongly:

'How else do you think? Because I'd met her daughter and heard the same tale she told you.'

'Where did you meet her?'

'That doesn't matter. The important point is that I did. I heard her name mentioned if you want to know, and it naturally struck me as being a coincidence. That was recently, after Kincaid returned, and before he pushed that man over Snowdon. From the first he'd been creating about his wife and trying to find out who she'd gone off with. And when I heard that name, immediately . . .'

'Was it Mrs Kincaid you expected to find?'

'Yes, it was. I was going to bribe her. I was going to get her to go back to Kincaid but to tell him nothing about being with Father. But as it turned out it was her daughter I met – my own half-sister, if you please! – and before I could work anything with her you'd arrested Kincaid for murder.'

'And you believed the girl's story, of course?'

'Good grief, and why shouldn't I? She doesn't know my name, so she could have no reason for lying to me.'

'You knew her real name was Phyllis Waters?'

'I knew she went under that name. But having two names is nothing: it's the usual thing with pros.'

'I notice you're familiar with their habits.'

Back flooded the embarrassment.

'All right, then . . . I'm not so innocent! My father didn't set a good example. But what does it matter? I heard her talked about . . . recommended; you can put it that way.'

'As Phyllis Waters?'

'No, Paula Kincaid! Why else do you think I went to see her?'

'On a recommendation.'

'Because of the name, I tell you.'

'Or because her youthfulness would fit the story.'

Askham was keeping his eyes blazing, but now he didn't find it so easy; they would like to have dropped before Gently's calm gaze. He could also sense Evans watching him, steadily, suspiciously, and Dutt's silent presence was somewhere behind his chair. He must have felt himself beginning to stare. He made a feint at rising.

'Look, if you're calling me a liar . . . !'

'Keep seated, Mr Askham.'

'In the first place, what right have you got; to order me about? You've none, and you know it.'

'We've a perfect right to ask you questions.'

'But not to call me a liar. And I won't stand for that.'

He was whipping himself up to a fresh pitch of indignation, perhaps even considering the possibility of flinging out of the room. He darted a glance at the door. Dutt absently changed his position. Gently swivelled his chair slightly so as to rest an elbow on the desk.

'Did you think we were going to believe it, a convenient story like that?'

'It's true. I know it's true. The girl told it me in good faith. I asked her casually about her people . . .'

'We can check her background quite easily.'

'But there's nothing one can check. And how could she have known about Paula Kincaid?'

'How indeed?'

'She couldn't, could she? I mean, the thing proves

itself. Either she *is* the woman's daughter or else it's all completely absurd.'

'Unless someone primed her, obviously.'

'But who would do a thing like that?'

'Someone very interested in Mrs Kincaid. Who wanted to keep her out of the hands of the police.'

'But that's ridiculous . . . I won't be accused! You can't be serious about this.' He was staring now and having to like it: the wind was going out of him fast. 'I tried to help you. It cost me money. I didn't care. I thought it was worth it. If you knew how it affected my mother . . . then, for you to turn on me like this!'

'Did your mother know about Phyllis Waters?'

'No – I told you! It would hurt her terribly.'

'Why are you so interested in Paula Kincaid?'

'I'm not. She's nothing . . . it's only Mother.'

'Yet your mother didn't seem so concerned.'

'She is. She doesn't show it, that's all.'

'How did you come to meet Arthur Fleece?'

Askham only stared. His lips were trembling.

An hour later it was bearing the marks of an all-night session, marks that Dutt understood well, though Evans still had to learn about them. Gently had sunk his teeth into Askham and time was no longer of any moment to him; he would go on and on now till he'd shaken the truth from the unlucky fellow. He'd made his mind up about Askham. That was the way Dutt read it.

And it was true. Gently could feel the ecstatic thrill of making contact. At last the fates had put in his hand one of the key figures of the enigma! Against the others he had been powerless, Kincaid, Stanley, Mrs Askham; Paula Kincaid was far to seek, Heslington he half believed in. But here, unsuspected and self-betrayed, was the weak link in the chain, and with him Gently could wrestle for the illuminating fact. Time was certainly no longer important. It was outside the reference of the problem. It was merely a symbol of infinity invoked to balance the equation.

'Where is Paula Kincaid now?'

He leant on the desk, his chin on his hands; his eyes were narrowed, his face a blank, he was questioning, questioning: one question after another.

'She's dead. You know she is.'

'Why don't you want us to find her?'

'How can you, when she's dead?'

'What did your father tell you about her?'

'Nothing. I tell you—'

'What does she know?'

'She's dead; you've got to believe her daughter—'

'What does she know about Met. L?'

'Nothing—'

'How much does your mother know?'

'Nothing! Except what she told you today.'

'It could have been lies. I'm asking you.'

'And I'm telling you, aren't I?'

'When did you last see Fleece?'

Askham's bearing was very altered now. That last disintegrating hour had ripped his veneer into tatters. From his pose as the heir to the Askham millions with power and influence behind him he had been reduced to a naked unit, clinging fearfully to his straw of innocence. He sat crumpled and flush-faced. His lips were dry, his eyes rolling.

'I . . . Fleece, I never met him.'

'He visited Paula Kincaid in Caernarvon.'

'He didn't . . . I mean, she's dead.'

'Why did he visit her?'

'He . . . but he didn't . . .'

'It had to do with Kincaid's return. It was dangerous to let her find him, wasn't it?'

'No, he couldn't, because she's dead.

'What makes you so certain. Have you some knowledge of her death?'

'Phyllis Waters . . .'

'She was lying.'

'No! She told you the truth about it.'

'She told me what you told her to tell me, and that's no answer. How much do *you* know?'

'Nothing. Only what she told me.'

'I'm beginning to think there's more to it than that. Like her having gone the same way as Fleece.'

'But that's crazy . . . you've got it wrong!'

'You're very insistent about her death.'

'She's dead, yes . . . but not like that . . .'

'Then suppose you tell me which way she died.'

'I can't. I only had it from Phyllis—'

'Think how tempting it would have been. To dispose of that dangerous woman for ever and to end her constant threat to someone . . . Then you could say she was killed in the blitz. You could produce a witness who we'd have to believe. Doesn't that sound like a clever way out, a safe way of guarding an ugly secret?'

'But it isn't true. You can't believe it—!'

'You'd be surprised what I have to believe.'

'I don't know anything about her death!'

'Then prove it to me. Where is Paula Kincaid?'

And so it went on, with never a break, chiselling and nagging at Askham's resistance; going round in circles, dragging in hypotheses, pounding away at any variation he introduced into his answers. Who could stand it for long without truth in his corner, or even so seconded? There came a time when it didn't matter . . .

Dutt, who'd heard it all and seen it all, retired to a seat in the corner, and there sought a sombre diversion in a file of *Police Gazettes*. Evans, new to the virtuosities of a full-dress Gently interrogation, continued to stare and digest in unconcealed admiration. It was going ill with the local wrongdoers when Evans returned to Caernarvon . . .

'Your mother knew Fleece, didn't she? She's apt to give herself away.'

'She didn't know him. She—'

'He paid her a visit when he went to see Paula Kincaid.'

'No – never!'

'I think he did. I think they had things to discuss together.'

'I tell you he's never set foot in Trecastles!'

'Where did they meet, then? In a hotel somewhere?'

'They didn't meet. We've never met him. What was a man like him to us? We didn't even know he existed . . . not till we read about him in the papers.'

'What did you read about him in the papers?'

'That he'd been . . . accidentally killed. And before that there was something else. He'd had a suit against Kincaid.'

'And, of course, you looked for items like that.'

'Yes, we did. My mother was upset.'

'Very natural that she should be. As the principal shareholder in Met. L.'

'But that has nothing—'

'Was it she who rang Fleece, or was it the other way about?'

'She'd *never* have rung Fleece!'

'Why not?'

'Because she . . . I've told you! She didn't know him.'

'So he must have rung her, and that started the acquaintance. He dashed across to Wales and they held a consultation. Paula Kincaid had to be dealt with; her husband was certain to catch up with her, and once he did then the fat would be properly in the fire. How did they plan to make her safe?'

'They didn't plan anything of the sort—'

'To move her was it? Send her abroad?'

'No . . . nothing. There weren't any plans . . .'

'To marry her maybe? Marry her to Fleece?'

'Oh, God!'

'Or perhaps to get rid of her entirely. Fleece was a man of resource in these matters: how much did he want to get rid of Paula Kincaid?'

He should have thought of it before: there was a certain relief from his torments. He could sit silent, letting the questions buzz harmlessly about his ears. It was a defeat, it vanquished the last shreds of the character he'd come in with, but it gave him pause from the destructive bombardment that was beating him to his knees. He summoned a defiant look for Gently: then he tightly closed his mouth.

'So that was the way of it, was it. Is that what you don't want to tell me?'

Gently noticed the change of reaction but seemed in no way concerned by it.

'Fleece was filing his divorce. That was a stage in plan one. But there was a later plan, plan two, devised to settle with Paula for good. She'd got the wind up about Kincaid. She couldn't be trusted to play her part. I can understand that you don't want to tell me, but you could put a finger on Paula's grave . . .'

'It's not true!' His silence was shattered by this intolerable insinuation; but he remembered himself directly and snapped his lips shut again.

'Why shouldn't it be true? It fits perfectly if you believe that Kincaid murdered Fleece. He was close on your trail over in Wales and might have got wind of what you were up to. That would make some sense of it, wouldn't it? Why he pushed Fleece over the Wyddfa?'

'Good gracious, man!' It was Evans who gave the reaction to that one. He began to rub his large hands, producing a dry, rasping sound. But Askham had retired into his shell.

His teeth as well as his lips were clamped. He stared hotly at Gently, an exhibition of determined silence.

'Then there's Heslington to consider.' Gently pressed on almost amiably. 'He was the man who

Fleece was citing, and he'd be sure to prefer Fleece dead. He'd be susceptibile to suggestion; you'd scarcely need to offer him a bribe. You'd show him your cards, you'd tip him the wink, and he wouldn't see too much on the Wyddfa. But what he did see would be carefully concerted to give support to a likely story.'

'He saw Kincaid and you know it!' Out, out it had to come. In spite of all the grinding of teeth, he had to respond when the chord was plucked.

'Yes, exactly; he saw Kincaid. And Kincaid has been the root of the trouble. A man who should never have returned from the dead and who it was desirable to reinter. Why shouldn't Heslington have seen him, if he saw anything at all up there?'

'But Kincaid . . . !'

'Has all sorts of motives. I know. They proliferate round the man. The more you look for them the more you find; you'd almost say he had too many. Because the murderer needed only one motive, one clear, sharp reason for giving that push. And he would need to be confident of his power to deliver it: one would have looked for somebody less frail than Kincaid.'

'But if he wasn't expecting it—'

'We think he was. We think he was face to face with his killer.'

'You don't know that!'

'We know a lot of things. And we'd like to know the whereabouts of Mrs Kincaid.'

It nearly did it. Askham was teetering, twice he was on the point of blurting it out. He tried to begin it a couple of times, his lips trembling and his eyes wild.

Then he seemed to rock away from it again; his face grew sullen and passionately hostile.

'She isn't anywhere. She's dead and buried. And not because anyone murdered her, either!'

Gently rose. He went over to the window. He stood staring out at the dark world of the Thames.

The break was for coffee and sandwiches; it had no other significance. Gently hadn't done with Askham; he'd hardly started on the fellow. Dutt had excused himself and gone, it wasn't his business anyway, and Evans, bursting for a discussion, was restrained by the presence of Askham. Consequently, he said nothing much, and Gently was far from being talkative. He sat broodily chewing his canteen sandwiches while apparently eyeing the marks on his blotter . . .

Yes, he'd only started with Askham; yet didn't he already have a part of the truth? Hadn't it begun to peer through the tangle during that first corrosive session?

Askham had conceded little in words but he had yielded much in the sum of his reactions. Time after time his temperature had risen when particular questions had been repeated. And the shape emerging from it was new – new and suddenly enlightening; it supplied the wanted touch of simplicity that Gently's instinct had predicted. But questions were unlikely to carry it further. They had done their duty in betraying the truth. A further session might confirm the pattern but he needed other artillery to achieve a breakdown. Questions were small-shot; the present occasion was calling for greater penetration . . .

He opened the Kincaid file and took out the O.S. map he had added to it. Askham, already reviving from his ordeal, watched it being spread out over the desk. Did he sense that something was decided, that a more searching test was being found for him; burning-cheeked, burning-eyed, the arrogance creeping back into his manner?

'Show me Trecastles.' Gently brought him into the act deliberately. Askham leaned forward. He pointed to the place with a finger that didn't tremble.

'Not far from Bangor, is it . . . ?'

'Bangor is just across the bridge.'

'How far are you from Caernarvon?'

'Eleven or twelve. I haven't checked it.'

There it lay in cartographical diagram, palely coloured, the drama's cockpit; the jaw of Anglesey, the blue serpent of Menai, and the club-footed sector with its ballast of Snowdon. There the flashpoint had occurred, the critical moment of these exchanges. On that spot upon the anvil had fallen the hammer of twenty-two years. And there one must go again, seeking the knowledge of that moment, assembling the actors, producing the play, forcing the drama to re-enact itself: stripping the thousands of possibilities from the one undoubted fact and making it stand there blazing naked: upon the summit waited the truth.

Evans was called to the phone and stood by it eating and chopping out monosyllables. Askham was gazing at Gently fixedly, watching where his eyes strayed on the map. Then, apparently by accident, their eyes came together, meeting and holding in a long caesura, holding till Askham dragged his away and let them sink to the map between them . . .

'Wait a minute, man. I'll jot that down.'

Evans juggled with the pad, the phone and his sandwich.

'And nowhere else . . . not in Caernarvon, say? Oh, very good, man . . . let me know the results.'

He stripped the sheet off the pad.

'So there's another thing settled. Fleece stayed each time at the same hotel: it was the St David in Beaumaris.'

'In Beaumaris?'

'Under his own name. Here are the dates on this paper.'

'Show it to Askham.'

Evans flipped the paper to the shrinking young man. Now his fingers trembled all right, he needed two attempts to pick up the sheet.

'What have you to say about that?'

'I . . . nothing! It doesn't mean . . .'

'It means that Fleece paid four visits to Beaumaris.'

'We didn't – we've never seen the man . . .'

It was a temptation to jump down his throat and to crush that lie flat, but Gently firmly resisted it. Not here, not yet!

'Very well, then. That's all – for this evening, in any case. But don't go off with the idea that we're satisfied with you.'

'I've told you everything . . . the truth!'

'Now listen carefully to what I'm saying. I want you to report at the police station at Llanberis at nine a.m. on Saturday.'

'B–but what for?'

'To assist the police.'

'I won't do it. You can't make me!'

Gently nodded his head steadily. 'You'll do it,' he said. 'Either I arrest you here and now on a charge of conspiracy, or you report at Llanberis at nine a.m. on Saturday. Which way do you want it?'

Askham didn't deign to answer. He glowered hate at Gently for a moment, then rose and hurled himself out of the office. They heard his feet patter down the stairs. Evans tipped the door shut behind him.

'Do you know, man,' he said pleasantly, 'I had an idea you'd be coming to Wales . . .'

CHAPTER ELEVEN

I T NEEDED A certain amount of staff work and a liaison with the Assistant Commissioner, a person who Gently preferred to avoid at this stage in a case. The A.C. was curious, rightfully curious, and he was the enemy of instinct and hunches; he had a pathetic faith in brute fact and in the validity of close reasoning. He had also a question which he deemed important:

'Have you identified Kincaid, Gently?'

It was naïve, but it required an answer, and then some time-wasting explanation.

'Let's get this straight, Gently! You can prove Kincaid is the man?'

Gently provided him with some brute facts and a modest garnish of close reasoning.

'Then why are you running off to Wales?'

In search of Mrs Kincaid, that was obvious. And taking in, for a *jeu d'esprit*, a reconstruction on Snowdon. Why was that? Gently was dour; he mumbled something about cigarette-cases. He added also, with engaging casualness, that powers of compulsion might be in request . . .

The latter were intended for Heslington's benefit, but in the event they proved unnecessary. After a serious chat on the phone with Gently, Heslington consented to appear at Llanberis. Overton needed no persuading, he sounded glad to be included, while a precautionary inquiry at Mount Street showed that the Askhams had left for Beaumaris. By Friday lunchtime the job was done and Gently and Evans were on the train to Holyhead.

They arrived late in Caernarvon and took a taxi direct to Evans's diggings. He had comfortable rooms in a terrace house that faced the low, green Anglesey shore. On their way there Gently had noticed that the streets were quite dry, and in the morning he found a Welsh sun bleaching the wide Menai flats. It was more than an omen: it was necessary. They needed the weather on their side.

'It should be clear at the top, man.'

Evans seemed a new man at breakfast. He had emerged from his London vapours and was wearing a face as bright as the sun. On the way down he'd had a spell of sulks; he'd tried and failed to draw the uncommunicative Gently; but now, with his foot under his native breakfast-table, he'd clearly dismissed the clouds from his nature.

'What a view, man. What a view to eat by.'

You might have thought he owned the Menai Straits. He sat Gently on the side of the table that faced them and kept giving him glances to be assured of his admiration. And he chaffed his landlady with an arch, sly wickedness. She was a comely forty-two. It was really too bad of him.

He had rung his station and a car arrived for them at half-past eight. It brought with it Sergeant Williams, a youngish detective with a serious face. Evans was now more on his dignity. His mien to Williams was stern. He checked critically on the sergeant's account of the investigations he had made locally. But there was nothing fresh to learn. Williams had uncovered no trace of Paula Kincaid. She wasn't a ratepayer, she hadn't voted, and she wasn't registered with the National Health Service; if in fact she'd been living in Caernarvon, it could only have been under a different name.

'Which is what one would have expected.'

Evans's spirits remained undampened. It was apparent that he was following a different line to Gently, and that his self-confidence was undisturbed by the odd freaks of the latter.

'We must look for a woman who left the town very suddenly. On Monday evening, or some time after that. She'll probably have left her things behind her; she'll just have packed a bag and gone. So it shouldn't be too difficult. There's probably people wondering already . . .'

Gently puffed his morning pipe without offering any comment. He watched the steaming, gold-green hills that began to appear on their right. He didn't want to talk, the time for discussion was over; he needed now to preserve the calm, the charged sensitivity of his mood. He was as an artist who had prepared his way and awaited the moment to pick up his brush. Nothing now must be allowed to divert him, to detract from that pregnant and dedicated poise . . .

They came to Llyn Padarn, looking cold and darkly blue, and then they were running into the countrified main street of Llanberis. It followed the trend of the district. It was narrow, crooked and strangely Victorian. Slate quarries frowned on it from across the llyn and folding mountains loomed ahead of it. And here it was that Kincaid had come in search of his wife, bridging two long decades with a tap on a door; noticing perhaps the new terraces which the quarriers had cut, and feeling once again the old lure of the mountains. Or so he had said, so ran his statement. And the truth was not now so very far off . . .

Outside the police station three cars were parked, one of them being Heslington's borrowed Austin-Healey. He sat in it reading a paper and wearing a surprisingly drab windcheater, but of course he was playing a different role: he was the Bearded Mountaineer. Near him stood Askham's red M.G., its owner lounging beside it, and an empty Vauxhall which no doubt belonged to Overton. The cast for the production were punctually assembled.

As they parked Heslington lowered his paper and saluted them with a scowl. Askham kept his back towards them; it was a trim back in a tweed sports jacket. They found Overton in the station chatting climbing with the inspector, and he sprang up smilingly as Gently entered. He offered his hand and a congratulation.

'You're lucky. This is just the weather we were getting on Monday. You could hardly have better in the middle of October.'

The inspector, a grey-haired man with a scar on his cheek, drew Gently to one side for a private confabulation.

'That young fellow out there. The one with the M.G.'

Gently nodded. 'I can guess. He's your Basil Gwynne-Davies, isn't he?'

'Oh, you know about him then?'

'We've begun to get acquainted. I'm hoping to know him rather better in a few hours' time.

'I'll wait, then. I thought I'd speak to you before I had him on the carpet.'

Overton also wanted a word. He'd been measuring Gently's build and dress.

'I don't know what you have in mind, but I'd recommend making the ascent from here.'

'We're taking the route from Pen-y-Pass.'

'Of course, if that's the one you want. Though if you aren't used to scrambles of this sort you'll find the Llanberis . . . well, less dramatic.'

'Thank you for the advice.'

'Don't think I'm trying to come the "old hand". But if you could borrow a pair of boots . . . and possibly a haversack and a sweater . . .'

They set out again in two cars, the one from Caernarvon and Overton's Vauxhall. In the boot of the former was a pile of gear which the Llanberis inspector had lent them. Gently had said nothing to Heslington or Askham – in fact, he'd said very little at all. Now he sat poker-faced and hunched, with even his pipe lying cold in his pocket.

* * *

At the Gorphwysfa Hotel at the head of Llanberis Pass they parked the cars beside a cart-track where the route to the Wyddfa began. As an introduction the road had been impressive. Mountains had risen steadily on each side of it. Particularly to the right, which was the Snowdon side, had the rock cliffs towered dizzyingly overhead. And now they were come to the top of the pass a wide valley opened below them, a vast concavity of sunlit space in the bottom of which there glittered a river. On the other side a road slanted to the south and seemed to have been scribed there with a tilted rule.

Evans had rung the hotel from Llanberis, so packs of sandwiches had been prepared for them. Gently donned his boots in the lounge. They were a formidable pair and were a size too large for him. His raincoat and sweater went into the haversack along with his sandwiches and a thermos of coffee. He felt, as he clumped outside again, a little ridiculous with his paraphernalia.

'Listen to me for a moment, then we'll be on our way.'

He could feel Overton eyeing him critically: his boots were probably laced up wrongly. Heslington's expression was faintly contemptuous, Askham was staring at the ground. Evans, in an undertone to Williams, was still laying plans for the apprehension of Mrs Kincaid.

'As you've been told, we're going to reconstruct what happened on the Wyddfa on Monday, or get as near to it as we can on the available information. We shall ascend by the route used by the majority of the club members and at the summit we shall re-enact what I think took place there. We are obviously short of some important people.' Gently paused to give emphasis. 'We're short of the victim, Arthur Fleece, and the man who has been charged with his murder. For that reason there will be stand-ins. Fleece I shall represent myself. And the place of Reginald Kincaid will be taken by Henry Askham.

'That's all. I would like you to lead the way, Mr Overton.'

Askham was facing him squarely now, if Gently wanted to catch his eye. He took a half-step forward, as though intending an angry protest. But Gently ignored him. He wouldn't even look. Settling his haversack on his shoulders, he tramped off heavily after Overton. Askham was left standing indecisively until a tap from Evans made him jump.

'You heard what the superintendent said, man?'

Askham got going with a toss of his head.

The cart-track was unsensational and appeared to descend rather than rise, giving no indication of how it was to reach the invisible summit. To the left the ground fell away without urgency into the valley, and ahead of them and to the right were grassy slopes on which sheep were feeding. A toy-like power station lay beneath them, fed by a plunge of organ-like pipes, and these alone, in their perfect recession, suggested a more impressive terrain beyond.

Their order of march seemed to fix itself

immediately. Overton went striding away in the lead. Gently came next, slouching in his mighty nailed boots, followed by Heslington, Askham, and the two local policemen. Heslington was keeping his distance deliberately; he dawdled along to prevent himself from catching up. In a similar way Askham was spacing himself behind Heslington, and behind him Evans and Williams went side by side. As odd a collection, surely, as ever climbed up Snowdon: and for as odd a reason as would ever be given.

Soon the track bore to the right and circled round Llyn Teryn, a small pool beside which stood some tumbledown cottages; then it bore right again, up a bit of steeper going, and then at last they had a prospect of what Snowdon kept in store for them. Overton waited for Gently and gave him a breakdown of the scene. The gaunt peak to the left of centre was indeed the mysterious Wyddfa. It was bounded on one side by the dark Lliwedd with its springlike veins of white quartz, and on the other by Crib Goch, a saw-edged razor against the sky. Under these lay Llyn Llydaw, a lake of long, wavy reaches, crossed below them by a granite causeway which had probably served the old copper mine. The ruins of the latter stood over the water. They looked grim and forlorn, a shattered venture.

'On the other side, you'll see, we shall begin to make some ground. We've been toying with it till now. We began at eleven hundred feet.'

Gently grunted, glad to rest his boots: he'd begun to wish he'd stuck to his brogues. The others were coming up the rise in a straggle with Evans and Williams well to the rear. They were talking animatedly together; Evans was making gesticulations.

'Is our time the same as yours was on Monday?'

Overton checked with his watch. 'A bit behind it, I'd say.'

'We'd better get on, then. I want the timing close.'

'It'll be all right. We started later on Monday.'

He lit a cigarette and then started off again. Gently followed. He let Overton lead by the same distance as before. Across the causeway they went, along the shore, past the desolate mine buildings; over increasing deserts of fallen rock and up a steady sharpening of the incline. Then again the swing to the right, getting brutally steep this time, with below to the left a whitened torrent that foamed down from the lonely Glaslyn. They were certainly making ground; Gently could scarcely keep pace with Overton. The shattered rocks were taking it out of him and making the sweat roll down his brow. And beneath them the llyn was falling away, and beside them the empty space grew emptier, encroaching upon his plainsman's resolve not to be intimidated by the mountains . . .

He was aware of feet scattering the rocks behind him and he turned to find Askham hard on his trail. The young man was also streaming with sweat and he had an expression which was far from happy. By a tremendous effort he got level with Gently. He turned to him an angry but apprehensive face.

'Why – why have we got to go up this way . . . ?'

They were both of them breathing very heavily.

Gently's boots were grinding and crashing as they laboured over the loose rocks.

'If I'd known, I wouldn't have come. They say . . . listen! They say it's worse further on. And the other way . . . why can't you listen? You could drive a car up the Llanberis track . . .'

Gently said nothing. He kept his face turned forward. Askham struggled to get ahead of him so that he could look at him by twisting his head back.

'It's stupid, I tell you . . . it's dangerous this way. People have been killed. There've been accidents here. And it's entirely unnecessary, you know it is! This isn't the way Kincaid went up . . .'

Gently's eyes remained averted. 'But it was Fleece's way,' he said.

'It wasn't.' Askham was furious. 'He used the Pyg Track, and you know it.'

'It joins this one higher up.'

'So does the track from Llanberis! This is dangerous, I tell you; it's only for people who're used to climbing . . .'

He lurched a little towards Gently; was it by accident that he was on the inside of him? A hundred feet or more below them the Glaslyn torrent curled over its rocks. But no, Gently pounded on his way, insensible and never wasting a glance; completely ignoring the desperate fear in the eyes that fought to engage his own. Askham stumbled, sobbing for breath.

'I won't – I won't come any further! I haven't got a head for heights . . . it makes me dizzy, I shall be sick. And you won't listen. It's no use talking to you. Oh, my God, why won't you listen? And you've dragged me into it for nothing . . . only because I tried to help you . . .'

He stumbled again, almost falling this time. He recovered his balance in a panic, shrinking closer to the wall of rock that hemmed the track at that point. There could be no doubt that he was really frightened; it wasn't a clever simulation. About his movements there was a tense automatism that betrayed the presence of physical fear.

'It's crazy . . . it's utterly pointless!'

Gently himself had a feeling of uneasiness. Somewhere, at a boundary that had passed unnoticed, the mountains had withdrawn their picturesque benevolence. They had begun to be wild, with an undertone of savagery; they seemed poised in a sinister potential of violence. Wherever one looked there were crushing rock-falls, unscalable cliffs, and hypnotic precipices. One experienced a sensation of being there on trial, of being small and alien and distinctly vulnerable . . .

'If anything happens, then you'll be responsible!'

Gently dashed at the sweat that lay heavy on his lids. Above them, standing easily with hands on hips, Overton rested and watched them as they laboured in the toils. One more bout and they would be there, another slam at that vicious incline! But already Gently's thigh muscles were crying for mercy, after only a foretaste of the scramble impending.

'If I get stuck you'll have to bring me down . . .'

Gently saved his breath and kept on slogging.

'I'll sue you, my God . . . I'll sue you!'

One last, killing stretch, and he stood shakily by Overton.

And then it was nearly worth getting up to that high vantage, worth it to peer into the inner recess which the mountain held concealed there. Level, shallow, grey, peaceful, the Glaslyn extended across its plateau, its ripples fretting the gentlest of music against its harsh rocky shore. Straight above it soared the Wyddfa, now more threatening than ever, its hollow cliffs of reddish grey exposed from their foot to their summit; and supporting them were high, frowning ridges that circled round the calm lake, leaving this rent through which spilled the torrent to join Llydaw, pale below.

'I'd sit a minute if I were you.'

Gently plumped down on a boulder. All right; he was turned fifty and not accustomed to these larks. Askham had already dropped prone and lay gulping his breath in fierce little gasps. Overton, casual and apparently sweatless, was lighting a fresh cigarette.

'Now you can see just where it happened. There's the Pyg Track. Can you make it out?'

Across the flank of the rightward wall one saw a scratched white line. Along there Heslington, and then Fleece, had taken their way to the ridge ahead, moving like tiny upright ants to the man who watched from the Glaslyn shore. Then up the ridge to the staring summit, that humpty cone with its sudden conclusion, the Tarpeian Rock: and the mortal cry as the human starfish floated down . . .

'You can see that apron-like projection? That's where he struck and started rolling. There was blood on it, quite plain. He couldn't have known anything after that. But he kept on tumbling down until he got there, where I'm pointing; and as you can judge, it was quite a feat to get across to him without equipment.'

'For God's sake stop it!' Askham sat up, his eyes burning at Overton. 'Don't you understand? Isn't it enough for me to be dragged up to this place . . . ?'

Overton turned to him in surprise. 'No offence intended, old man.'

'There is offence. I can't stand it. This bloody mountain is driving me crazy!'

He jumped to his feet and jerked away from them, to throw himself down again at a distance. Overton stared bewilderingly at Gently. He was wholly taken aback by the explosion.

'What's needling the youngster?' he wanted to know.

Gently gave a lift of his shoulder. 'It's just the mountains,' he replied. 'They have an effect on some people.'

Had he ever been as tired and perhaps so fundamentally frightened? He didn't know and daren't think about it, caught in the dizzying web of the Zigzags. After the first few hundreds of feet he had begun to feel a slow panic, and all the way after that he'd had to fight it with his will. It was absurd. There was no danger, it was only the scale of the thing that sapped at him. The side of the ridge was no steeper than a house roof and was gnarled with helpful outcrops of rock. If he'd slipped and fallen he wouldn't have rolled far, would perhaps have come off with the shock and some bruises; while

189

at the worst – say, a broken leg – he had experienced companions to come to his aid. Yet still he couldn't get rid of that panic, he could only oppose it and keep it under: by not looking back, down seven hundred feet; by not looking up, another five hundred. From minute to minute, just the rock-rim ahead . . .

Overton, mercifully, was staying down close to him. He was gruesomely enjoying this swing up the ridge. He climbed with a relaxed and familiar rhythm and apparently took nothing out of himself at all. He could even find time to make a little conversation. The Wyddfa, it seemed, resembled Everest in miniature. The chasm below them would represent the Western Cwm, the Crib-y-ddysgl Lhotse, and the ridge the South Col.

'And under snow the resemblance must be even more striking. In January now . . . I've a good mind to try it in January.'

But Overton, roving on in front, then dropping back to keep touch, wasn't sticking so near to Gently as was Henry Askham. The latter had made his attachment permanent and went beside Gently like his shadow; grey of face, drenched with sweat and his hair plastered damply over his brow. He hadn't ventured a word since that outburst down below. He'd kept his distance while the others arrived and while Gently had given a few instructions. But directly the party moved he had scrambled up to join the detective, his eyes averted and mouth gone small, his head and shoulders drooped a little. And so he had stuck, a spaniel at heel, enduring the terrors of the Zigzags . . .

Of the others, Gently noticed that Heslington had dropped his earlier aloofness. He was now accompanying Evans and Williams and was seemingly on terms not uncordial. Gently saw them below him, now strung out, now proceeding together in a knot, and twice he heard Evans's laugh and the sudden lilting rise of his voice. They were used to it of course, the three who followed on behind. Two of them were born in the shadow of Snowdon; this was like a stroll up their own backyard.

'Here would be about the spot, Super.'

Overton halted by a marker cairn. He took his bearings across the void with a callous sang-froid that made Gently shiver.

'You see? There's Crib Goch just on a level, and the Moel Siabod in line beyond it; roughly we're on the twenty-eight hundred mark. I was near a marker when I heard the cry.'

Gently dropped on his hands and knees and seated himself before looking; to rest his legs, it might have been, they were surely in need of it! Then he braced himself for the survey, taking a firm grip on his nerves. Below his boots he caught sight of the Glaslyn, now turned hard and very steely-looking . . .

'Do you hear those choughs. The way they echo?'

He could hear them all right, and he wished he couldn't. Two wavering black dots passing slowly across the summit, their choking cries seemed to rake at his viscera.

'So now you can imagine—'

'There's no need to be explicit.'

191

And Askham too was clearly of Gently's opinion. He was lying face inwards, his hands grasping the rock, and he gave a whimpering kind of groan as he heard Overton's commencement.

'How are we doing for time?'

'We'll be up there soon after one. You wouldn't like me to speed it up a bit, would you?'

Gently echoed Askham's groan. 'I was born in a flat country!'

'You'll like it when we get on the ridge. You'll find it a different world up there.'

A minute of rest, no more: not even time for their sweat to dry, though the sun was falling hotly on the south-facing slope; then they were up and on again, pursuing the goat-like stride of Overton, with the loose rock scuttling from underfoot and the live rock making them check and stagger. Was there no end to those punishing Zigzags, no ultimate rock-rim above which was no other; were they doomed now until life was extinct to continue agonizedly climbing into a perpetual extension? Askham's distress was even greater than his own. He had got to a state where he no longer dared to rest. He simply kept going in a panic-triggered scramble, with the knowledge of the void behind him staring from his eyes. The problem had gone to the mountains again, and the mountains were ready with their answer . . .

And finally they could see it, the true ridge-top fretted above them; about a hundred feet higher and the last fifty of them sheer and smooth. But Overton was bearing to the right now; he was making a long, shallow traverse, bringing them safely to a low gap by which the ridge-top was easily attained. He stood watching them clinically as they came over; he had a caustic look for Askham. The youngster dropped as though he were shot as soon as he staggered out of the gap. Gently's knees were shaking too; the relief of getting up there was tremendous! But he managed to clump a few steps from the gap before he permitted those knees to collapse. Then he sat motionless, his arms hanging limp, drinking in the sweet, cold breeze of the top.

'There you are. How's that for a prospect?'

Overton was ruthless, he was a bundle of springs. He pointed to Llanberis, Caernarvon, Anglesey, Tremadoc Bay, and the ghost of Liverpool.

'Isn't it something, though you only get this far?'

Gently accepted the disparagement without a murmur. Askham to all intents was dead to the world. He lay with closed eyes and his cheeks had a leaden colour.

And so they were mustered for the last lap, on what seemed the backbone of the world: the titanic ridge that climbed from Llanberis up to the highest level of all. To right and left the great spaces fell away in soaring chasms of light and colour, leaving their knife-edge rising inexorably, straight and firm towards the summit. Heslington went first, as he had done on the Monday, his manner and step determinedly jaunty; Gently came next with Askham at his elbow, and the other three silently followed behind. Silently, because there was an atmosphere somehow, a peculiar tenseness that quelled their chatter; so that even Evans, now confessedly in opposition, was catching the faint echo of a drama unexpressed. After all, was there more in Gently's whims than met the eye . . . ?

Askham was almost touching Gently, so near was he trudging along beside him: that was the point that kept striking Evans on the slog up the ridge. At the bottom Askham had been rebellious, he'd been furiously angry with Gently, but now he slunk at the Yard man's side, a chastened, almost a filial figure. What had happened between them coming up? Evans wished he'd kept a more attentive eye on them. All he'd noticed was that Askham was panicky and had obviously a shocking head for heights. But that didn't explain this turnabout from angry antagonism to servile deference, nor the little glances that Askham kept throwing at Gently's unregistering, rock-like face . . .

Evans muttered at last to Overton: 'What did they talk about man, him and Askham?'

Overton raised and let fall his hands. 'Nothing. Though the young man was blowing off steam.'

'It was only that? It was nothing more?'

'Nothing that I heard in any case. There wasn't a lot of conversation after we'd started on the Zigzags.'

So the mystery continued a mystery and Evans frowned as he strode along.

Now the café appeared ahead, hopefully crowning the last long slope, an ugly, utilitarian building on the lines of a mess-hut from a temporary camp. They saw Heslington work his way towards it, pass across the front and disappear; providing a positive demonstration of the tenability of his story. Thus the scene was set as on Monday, with the time at precisely five minutes past one. The sun, as then, stood over the summit and was full in their eyes as they approached. Gently halted when they drew near the café.

'One of you – Williams – remain here, will you? I want you to keep your eye fixed on the top there, above the café. Is that understood?'

'Yes, sir.' Williams stiffened himself involuntarily. 'But what do you want me to watch for, sir?'

'For whatever you can see. And remember, it's important. So don't let your attention wander for a second.'

Leaving Williams looking puzzled, they proceeded to the café, which lay niched into the rock on the right, its roof on a level with the track. Above it to the left stood the round cairn, a drum-shaped platform of rocks, a matter of thirty feet in diameter and ten or twelve in height. The track passed round it, still screwing upwards, to end in a sloped plane of rock which was the summit. From the base of the cairn to the brink of this platform would be a distance of perhaps fifteen yards.

Gently brought them to a stand again on the far side of the cairn, not sufficiently advanced round it to have re-entered Williams' field of vision. For several moments he stood studying the disposition of the spot, the cairn, the narrowing slope and the violent emptiness it descended into. Then he felt in his pocket and – for the first time – turned to Askham.

'Take this.'

It was the cigarette-case bearing the monogram

'RTK'. Askham drew his breath sharply. He visibly shrank away from Gently.

'I . . . no! Why should I – why are you giving that to me?'

'Take it!'

The case was shoved into his reluctant hand.

'Now . . . !' Gently's voice sounded softer, his lids sank a little. 'I shall need some help from you in your capacity of Kincaid. He was evidently up here ahead of Fleece, and perhaps ahead of Heslington too. But he wasn't concealed behind the café, because Heslington went there to eat his lunch. Yet Fleece didn't see Kincaid when he was coming up the track, so he must have been somewhere not immediately visible. I'd like you to suggest where that somewhere could have been, where Kincaid could see Fleece, but Fleece missed seeing Kincaid.'

It was too simple. There was only one place. Askham pointed to it tremblingly.

'Yes . . . you're probably right. It was up there on the cairn. So will you take your place there?'

'I . . .' Askham's look of appeal was pitiful.

'Just climb up the cairn, please. Stand at the back, where it's highest.'

Still he lingered, as though in hope of a reprieve from Gently's fiat; but there was no more prospect of that than of the Wyddfa beginning to melt. He clambered unsteadily on to the cairn.

'Kincaid was sitting down, wasn't he . . . ?'

Askham sat, he nearly fell. He crouched with head sunk forward on his chest.

'Right . . . now we're getting somewhere. We'd better hear what Williams can tell us.'

Evans stepped back round the cairn and whistled through his fingers for the sergeant. Williams appeared, rather out of breath, apparently having read urgency into the signal. But Gently didn't seem in a hurry.

'What did you see from back there?'

'I saw Askham on the cairn, sir. At least, I did when he was standing up.'

'But when he was sitting?'

'Well then I might perhaps have seen his head, sir. But with the sun in my eyes, I wouldn't like to be certain.'

'It was a sunny day on Monday.'

Gently's eyes never left Askham. If he'd ignored him before he was paying the debt now with interest.

'The rest of you wait here, will you?'

He turned his back on the cairn. He began to walk down the slope towards the edge of the abyss. Slowly, but with steps that didn't hesitate, giving no indication of his purpose, he continued down to the last treacherous footing of loose rock. And there he remained, for several seconds, while Evans could feel his blood run chill: a hunched-up figure, hands in pockets, framed in the void that extended beyond Snowdon. At the end of that interval he turned again. But he moved not a step away from the edge.

'Stand up, Askham. Take out the case I gave you.'

Askham had been watching too. Now he could scarcely get to his feet. He fumbled impotently for the case, which after all was in a different pocket. He held it out quiveringly, as though expecting Gently to take it.

'Now light a cigarette.'

Wasn't it asking too much? Even picking one from the case seemed an act beyond his power. The matches scattered through his fingers, he struck a couple that blew out. He got a fag lit at last, but looked unable to keep it going.

And then there was chaos.

Gently screamed; his feet thrashed wildly for a foothold. His arms flew up in a desperate windmill and the loose rock scattered from his frenzied boots. It was all so sudden, there was nothing one could do. Everything else was in slow motion . . . before they could reach him the inevitable happened; he lost his balance and pitched down headlong on the rocky slope of the Wyddfa summit.

The effect was appalling, no less on the others as on Askham. In a concerted rush they had sprung down the slope and now were laying panic-stricken hands on Gently. But he was up directly, thrusting them aside, striding back and up on to the cairn, to the sobbing young man with his spilled cigarette-case and the fallen cigarette, lighted ten seconds earlier.

'*And what happened then?*'

Askham's state was deplorable, he couldn't get out as much as a croak. He stood swaying, blubbing, shaking like an aspen; pushing out a feeble hand towards Gently. On all of Snowdon they stood, the two of them, looking down on two countries: the implacable man who would have the truth and the defenceless youth who couldn't speak it.

'I d–d–d–didn't . . . !'

His teeth were chattering, his lip kept getting in the way.

'I d–d–didn't push him . . . I w–wouldn't have dared . . . I'd never have gone down where he was . . . !'

'Then why did he fall?'

'He h–heard me . . . saw me. He was st–standing like you were, looking down at the view. And then I got up and he turned round and saw me . . . he must have thought . . . and then he l–l–lost his balance . . .'

'What was it he thought?'

Askham gave a great shudder. 'He knew I wanted him . . . w–wanted him dead . . .'

'*And what was the reason for wanting him dead?*'

The stammer sank to a whisper. 'Blackmail . . . *dirty blackmail . . . !*'

The last two words were barely audible, but they seemed to go echoing down the Wyddfa cliffs.

CHAPTER TWELVE

BLACKMAIL: DIRTY BLACKMAIL. Dispelling Kincaid like a mist, banishing him precipitately from the Wyddfa and back to the probable truth of his statement. It was a bitter moment for Evans as he stood staring at the two on the cairn, a moment of personal revelation which he was too honest to avoid. Out of some different level of understanding Gently had produced this confounding trump card.

'Then *he's* the one who Heslington saw!'

It had perforce to be more of a statement than a query. Once you had grasped the basic fact, the details went tumbling into place. Askham's height came near to Kincaid's. His build, his carriage were much the same. Glimpsed from the back at a suitable distance, he would easily pass muster for the man himself. Another point that Evans had missed.

'Right. We may as well have our meal.'

Gently was climbing down from the cairn with a bland inconsequence of expression. But surely he hadn't done questioning Askham, when there was so much still to be explained! All the background to that mysterious blackmail, with its deep-set roots and weary entanglements? And at the very least:

'Won't you charge him, man?'

'With what?' Gently stared at him blankly.

'Why . . . I'd say . . .' Evans floundered uncomfortably, feeling more and more left out of the picture.

It was a curious meal, the one they ate there, with the Olympian view rolled out beneath them. Except for Heslington, who had missed that scene, nobody had much to say for themselves. And Heslington too soon gave up trying. He could sense that something climactic had occurred. He put out feelers to Overton to find if he, Heslington, were affected, then decided that he wasn't and got on with his sandwiches. All along there had been a growing air of confidence about Heslington.

More remarkable to Evans was the tie between Gently and Askham, which continued unaffected by the passage of the thunder. The young man had sat down by him still trembling from his ordeal, but he was soon showing more composure, and with it a sort of tremulous regard. Evans felt a twinge of jealousy; *he* was being ignored by Gently! He was at a loss to find a reason for the irritating phenomenon. In his experience there was little love lost between a chummie and his apprehender, especially when the chummie had been given a dose of treatment like this one.

'I didn't know . . . it was Kincaid . . .'

Askham had started to mutter something. He swooped on a thermos to pour some coffee for Gently.

'Down in Llanberis I asked them . . . so I thought he'd come here. I had to see him of course . . . and that was the reason . . .'

And Gently grunted as though it made sense, reaching his hand for the coffee. What had happened? At what point had Evans gone off the road?

After the meal it became increasingly plain that Gently had finished for the present; as of then, the whole excursion might have been a pleasure trip. With Askham slinking in his wake and Overton providing information, he made an appreciative circuit of the top, asking nothing but tourist questions. Then he was ready to go down; he had exhausted the Wyddfa. That single blaze of illumination was apparently all he asked from it. He had somehow been able to foretell it and now he'd got it he was satisfied. It clicked home. Evans knew instinctively that Gently had the whole story.

Did it hinge on what Kincaid knew about the incident on Everest, and Harry Askham's part in that? Could the answer be so simple?

On the long, dull descent to Llanberis, only a moorland track below Clogwen Bridge, Evans wrestled unceasingly with the problem, giving it all the benefit of his needle-bright logic. He wanted so badly to get there himself, to reach the answer before Gently came out with it; and it had to be staring him in the face somewhere, since he knew the facts as well as the Yard man. Yet the more he grappled with them the more stubborn they became. Without further investigation there seemed no prospect of squaring them. Behind any blackmail must lie a secret, and that secret was buried deep; known perhaps by the Askhams, mother and son, but only certainly by the Kincaids. And not knowing that how could one be so smug and so oracularly self-satisfied as Gently? Or, what was worse, so infuriatingly right? The facts stretched like a wall against any such certainties.

And he was still butting his head against it when they straggled down to the town, past the outlying houses and bungalows and on to the welcoming metalled road. Had he begun to suspect its significance, to plot its position in the Gentlian process; to sense that it was here Gently had turned his back when that wall insisted on barring his way . . . ? He was staring at Gently very hard. But he was much too proud to ask a question.

'Where's the best place to eat in Llanberis?'

Gently was dragging his boots with fatigue. Evans observed it with a consoled satisfaction: here was something Wales had taught the maestro!

'The Snowdon Café is as good as anywhere.'

'Right. We'll go there straight away.'

'What about . . . ?' Evans motioned to Askham.

'He'll come along too. Do you think he climbs on air?' Evans had a savage glance for the young man but he said no more. It was Gently's party!

After climbing on sandwiches, one ate like a tiger. That was the immediate lesson that Wales had taught Gently. His body craved food, its furthest extremities cried out for it, and for forty-five minutes he did nothing but empty plates. Then he sighed and felt for his pipe. There was something to be said for climbing mountains! He took a few luxurious puffs before running an eye round his company.

'I'd like to thank those present for giving me their assistance.'

Was it spoken as a dismissal? Nobody seemed eager to take it up. A subtle bond was linking them together, the unspoken friendship of the hills. It had grown there unawares and had suddenly surprised them with a unity, setting the disparate aside, making evens of the odds. Heslington was the first to speak.

'Then I can take it you've finished with me?'

'Yes, I think so.'

'If you don't mind, I should like to have it a little more definite. At one stage you came near to accusing me, not without grounds, I'm ready to admit. And I want to make sure that you're satisfied now.'

'Quite satisfied, Mr Heslington.'

'And Sarah. I can tell her?'

Gently nodded, blowing smoke. 'We shan't be troubling Mrs Fleece.'

'In that case . . .' Heslington stood up. He felt in his hip pocket for his wallet. 'I'll be getting on the road. I want to be back in town tonight.'

He went, with a nod to Overton, his red head jerking when he strode past the window; in the final analysis unexpectedly impressive and with a dignity seen to be sincere. Had he been a red herring? No: not quite. He had held a key piece in that intricate jigsaw. A few moments later they saw him pass in the sports car, but his eyes were fixed on the long road ahead.

'I suppose that goes for me too.'

Overton's smile was lazy, and after stretching and flexing his arms he let them drop with a grunt. But he wasn't tired; you could tell that. His sallow skin gave the wrong impression. The mountain that had squashed Gently flat was only a loosener to Overton.

'Of course, I'd like to tag along and get to the bottom of this lark, but I only came for the ride, so I'd better follow Ray's example. Only my car is up the pass.'

'Sergeant Williams will find you transport.'

'Well, I can't say I'm not baffled. But I've enjoyed the trip all the same.'

He rose, Williams with him; but Gently detained them with a gesture.

'Just one more question. This one comes from my superior at the Yard. Why do you people want to climb Everest?'

'Why?' Overton's brown eyes danced at him. 'But I should be here all night if I even started to answer that.'

'In a couple of words, though?'

'You'd think me a fool if I told you.'

'I won't show it.'

'All right, then! It's to get at the soul of the beast.'

And he ducked away from an explanation, towing Williams along after him.

Then they were three; Evans, Gently, Askham sitting in sulky thought, his head bowed over his coffee, his hands clasped under the table. The culprit, if there was a culprit, and Evans very much wanted to think so. But more likely the tormented inheritor of a harrowing patrimony.

He made a last half-hearted effort.

'My car is here . . . can't I go too?'

Gently sternly shook his head. 'You're coming back to Caernarvon with us.'

'You can't make me. I haven't been charged.'

'I'll soon do that if you'd prefer it. Otherwise you'll come with us. We haven't quite finished yet.'

His head drooped over the cup again.

'You're going to talk to my mother, aren't you?' he mumbled.

It was the same in Wales as in London or in any other police station on earth; the same tidy untidy room with its desk and chairs and filing cabinets. The same smell of floor polish and paper and tobacco smoke that was never dispersed, the identical dingy painted walls, brown linoleum, and tin waste box. All that was different in Evans's office was the calendar pinned behind the door, which was issued by a Welsh firm with an unpronounceable name and which carried a picture of a Welsh girl in national costume. But the atmosphere was correct. It touched its chord of condemnation.

'I must admit I was surprised, Superintendent.'

She had swept in finely with her surge of hauteur; driving the atmosphere back with her presence and filling the office with her own. Then she had seen her son, and stopped, making her stand-out skirt rustle. She had fixed her eyes accusingly on his hunched and shamefast shoulders.

'Oh I see. It's about Henry, is it. I wondered why

you had fetched me out here. And what has my son been up to this time: another car-smash, is it?'

'Please sit down, Mrs Askham.'

'I'm hoping it won't be necessary, Superintendent. If it's a question of bail we can settle that immediately, and since I have guests to dinner, I should prefer not to be detained.'

'It isn't a question of bail.'

'Not bail. Is it something troublesome?'

'I'd sooner you sat down, Mrs Askham. It has to do with Reginald Kincaid.'

'That man. So that's it.'

She gave her son a harder look. But he was determinedly turned away from her, his face towards one of the filing cabinets.

'Very well, then. I'll sit down. I didn't know we were still on that business. But you will do me a favour, Superintendent, by being as brief as you possibly can.'

She was indeed dressed for dinner and she arranged her billowing skirt with care. She was wearing a gown of pale straw and pearls gleamed dully above its neckline. About her shoulders was a quilted wrap in her especial tint of lilac, and she wore long matching gloves and lilac shoes with incredible heels. Her hair was sculptured rather than brushed and she wore in it a golden, pearl-studded comb.

Gently was cautious with his opening.

'I'm trying to complete our knowledge of the case. We still need some details about Fleece and Kincaid with reference to the time when you engaged Paula Kincaid. I thought you'd be the person best able to help us.'

'I see. But what has this to do with my foolish son?'

'Your son has been helping us, Mrs Askham. He had some information to give.'

'About Kincaid?'

'About Kincaid. And a few collateral matters.'

'My son is imaginative, Superintendent.'

'We have had occasion to notice that.'

Her eyes had their usual frigid boldness but it was now a little icier, a little harder. They had been fencing from the outset and she was perfectly aware of it. She had no nerves. She knew her strength. She was a perfect mistress of her weapon.

'Very good. Then what are your questions?'

'Two of them relate to sums of money. The first concerns the ten thousand pounds with which your husband financed the expedition to Everest.'

'My husband did no such thing.'

'But Harry Askham paid that money.'

'Then it was done without my knowledge.'

'Why was that, Mrs Askham?'

She made the gesture of flicking her skirt. 'I wouldn't necessarily know. I think I told you before that I didn't meddle with my husband's business. He was quite generous with his charities.'

'Even when they were anonymous?'

'He could also be disinterested.'

'Surprisingly so, it would seem.'

She let the thrust go by her. 'And there was a second sum of money?'

'Yes.' Gently hit the word hard. 'Another disinterested donation. We haven't obtained the figures for this one but it would need to be in the tens of thousands. And it was paid to Arthur Fleece. On his successful return from the expedition.'

'That I consider to be absurd.'

'I quite agree. Unless it had a motive.'

'There could be none.' Her chin was up, she let her eyes sweep him witheringly. 'Wherever this man obtained his money, I can assure you it was not from Harry, Harry had obligations to nobody. Certainly not to a sacked employee.'

'Fleece was sacked?'

'So I understood. I remember it being mentioned at the time. Some dishonesty in his records. I don't remember precisely what.'

'Then there would be a record of that at Metropolitan Electric. Some of the staff would remember the incident.'

'They might.' She picked a thread from her skirt. 'But then again, it was probably hushed up.'

Gently's nod was caustic. 'I feel sure it would have been. The air at Hendon seems to have a relaxing effect on memories. But you knew nothing of this payment?'

'Nothing whatever. It was never made.'

The foil was handsome, but that didn't betray her into complacency. From the height of her expensive presence, she continued to eye him with alert attention. Henry Askham had straightened a little as though perhaps taking courage from his formidable mother. Evans was sitting in a crouching attitude. He seemed holding himself to spring on something or somebody.

'I'd like you to consider those two payments

together and in conjunction with what happened on Everest. I think you will come to a certain conclusion. I think your son has already done so.'

'I didn't know—!'

Askham flung round, a truly ghastly look on his face. He stared in horror at his mother, who regally inclined in his direction.

'Henry. You'd better leave the talking to me.'

'But you don't understand! I had to tell him—'

'You are over-imaginative, Henry.'

'But this . . . this . . . !'

'You must control your nerves, boy. You should try to be more reserved in public. Superintendent, you will kindly excuse him. As an only son he's been spoiled, I'm afraid.'

Askham groaned and pulled away from her. She sat still and unmoved. Her hands lay quietly on her lap and the muscles of her mouth were unstressed. After a moment she resumed calmly:

'I missed the point of your last question. I thought that what happened on Everest was beyond any sort of proof.'

'You are familiar with accounts of it, then.'

'Oh yes. Is that discreditable?'

'And with the version Kincaid gave?'

'One could scarcely escape that.'

'How would you interpret it, Mrs Askham?'

'I'm not certain that I want to. But if it were proved, then I should say Kincaid had reason to murder Fleece.'

'You may take it as being proved.'

'Oh, really?' Her chin was lifting again. 'Then a

conviction is almost certain. I suppose I should congratulate you, Superintendent.'

'And those two sums of money are proved. Your husband paid for that expedition. And he paid Fleece when he returned. And he caused Paula Kincaid to vanish.'

'You are wrong. Completely wrong.'

'And Fleece knew something else, didn't he? Your husband went for a ride on a tiger, and the tiger came back: he came *for you*.'

'Stop it . . . stop it!' Henry Askham sprang up, his eyes wild and his hair dishevelled. 'I can't stand it, I tell you, I can't! I shall go mad . . . you've got to stop it!'

'Henry.' Her voice cut like a knife.

'And you. You. You knew all about it! Knew that Father – oh, my God! I can't stand it – I shall go mad!'

'Henry, be silent.'

'I can't . . . I can't!'

'You will control yourself this moment.'

'I'm finished. I just can't take it.'

'It isn't true, Henry. *It isn't true.*'

Neither of them had seen Gently's finger on the bell-push, nor noticed the door swinging silently open. He came in looking perplexed, his intense eyes switching about him, the brown suit he'd worn in the cells crumpled and badly needing a press. Then he heard the voice of the seated woman. His eyes grew wide, he began to tremble. He took a stumbled step forward and gave a little sobbing cry.

'Paula . . . *Paula!*'

Mrs Askham whirled to her feet. He was standing with his hands outstretched towards her.

Was it altogether real, the tableau enacting in that room, painfully extending itself to moments, a scene in which every actor had dried? The spindly man with his appealing hands and tears rolling down his cheeks, the thunderstruck woman with ghost-seeing eyes, the staring young man backed against the cabinet? It seemed to hang breathlessly on the brink of unbeing, as though a sudden movement might sweep it away: dissolved and cut by its own emotion like a celluloid shadow from the screen.

Then slowly Mrs Askham turned her back on Kincaid.

'Paula!'

The movement drew him after it. But he seemed to be shackled, he could advance only one foot. He stopped. He became as motionless as before.

'Paula. Oh, look at me!'

She wouldn't. Her face was bitter. She wasn't seeing Gently, though her eyes faced straight towards him.

'Paula, I love you. It's never changed. I love you, Paula. I love you!'

Her mouth opened before she spoke. Finally she said:

'It's no use, Reg.'

'But, Paula, I love you. I want you!'

'No, Reg. It's no use.'

'Paula, listen to me. I'm rich now . . .'

Her lips twisted. 'And I'm poor!'

'It doesn't matter.' He came another step. 'I'm rich, Paula. Don't you hear? We've got money now. A hundred thousand! I brought it back with me from Tibet.'

A hundred thousand . . . ! Gently saw the pitying expression that passed over her face. What was a hundred thousand to Mrs Askham: would it melt one splinter of her ice? She'd tossed the sum away on trifles, some fresh bloodstock, a new yacht; and that little man in his scrubby suit thought he was going to tempt her with such a bagatelle! The anger blazed. She swung on Kincaid:

'Are you blind to what you've done?'

'Paula . . . !' Her rage pushed him backwards, his lips quivered and fell dumb.

'Don't you realize you've made me a pauper – me, a millionairess; stripped this very gown from my back; taken the ring off my finger?'

'But Paula, listen . . .'

'Listen. Listen! Will that do any good now? Will it make me Harry's widow again? Confirm my title to his estate? You've ruined me, Reg, that's what you've done. You've practically tossed me into the street. And now you insult me with your pretty charity, your childish sentiment and your hundred thousand! What must I do about it – kiss you? Throw my arms round your neck?'

'Paula . . . I don't understand . . .'

Her savage laugh made him wince.

'Don't you? But Dicky Askham will understand, and so too will his lawyers. I had to fight that wastrel before, Reg. He contested the will right through the courts. And what sort of case do you think I'll have now – as Harry's mistress, with Henry his bastard? I'll be fortunate to get a pittance: a beggarly percentage of your wonderful fortune. And Harry's son can sweat in the works while his uncle squanders his father's money . . . ! And you've done it by walking in here, Reg, only by looking at me and saying, 'Paula.' Paula was dead and Paula was buried – and you, you're the stranger who's made me poor!'

She flung away again with vehement passion, her eyes sparkling and blind. Kincaid stood as though entranced; crushed, broken by her piercing anger. For several seconds he couldn't speak. He seemed to have died inside his body. Then insensibly something began to return, the lamp of his glazed eyes lit again.

'Paula . . .'

Her shoulders snatched at him, willing him to have done.

'Paula, I didn't know . . . I couldn't guess that I would do you an injury.'

'But you have, Reg. And I hate you for it.'

'No, Paula. You mustn't hate me.'

'But I do. I do.'

'You're angry with me. Only angry.'

She stamped her foot, and to Gently's surprise he could see a tear trembling under her lashes. But her lips were pressing tight and her chin thrust well forward.

'I want you to go now, simply go.'

'Not without you, Paula. Never.'

'Reg, you must.'

'Don't ask it of me. I love you, Paula. You're all my life.'

'I've not been faithful.'

'I understand that.'

'You must suspect me.'

'No. I can't.'

'I'm a hard bitch, Reg. You can ask my son,'

'You're Paula Kincaid. You're my wife.'

What had come over him? He had suddenly transcended the eccentric character by which they had known him; even his voice had a deeper tone and his weedy figure appeared more substantial. And as his stature grew, Mrs Askham's lessened, her commanding presence was whittled away. From being a priceless doll with a vice-royal manner, she was rapidly diminishing into something like a woman . . .

'Listen, Paula. Why is this money important? What have you ever bought with it that has helped you to be happy? Has it made people love you? Has it made you less lonely? Has it stood to you as a husband since the man who took you died? If I've lost that for you, I've brought you something else, Paula. I've brought you a love that's never altered, through all the bitter times past. And I've all the money we can ever need, more than we need with each other. Then why is your money so important? Why does losing it seem so hard?'

'It's no use, Reg; we're strangers. You don't know me now.'

'I *do* know you.' He came closer, standing right by her side.

'I'm unforgivable. I know that.'

'No, Paula. You're always forgiven.'

'I've got to hate you . . .'

'You can't do it.'

'I *must* hate you. I *must* . . .'

Then the tears came. Quietly, without any sobbing. Making her feel unseeingly for her handkerchief to dab to her eyes.

'You're not to touch me,' she said. 'You're not to touch me, Reg . . .'

She didn't break down at all. But that would probably come later.

CHAPTER THIRTEEN

I N THE MIDDLE of the proceedings arrived the Caernarvonshire Chief Constable, who had been warned by his spies that some development was afoot. He was a tall ex-Army man and the owner of a finely waxed moustache, and he evidently knew Mrs Askham and looked rather perturbed at finding her there. She gave no sign of knowing him, however; it was left to Evans to acknowledge his entry. Then after some whispering he took a chair in the background, there to make what he could of the goings-on.

Gently was questioning; that was inevitable. His slow, flat voice laid query to query. He was covering ground unfamiliar to the Chief Constable and having apparently small connection with Fleece's murder. Really, the only suggestion of it was the presence of Kincaid; and that alone brought a frown to the Chief Constable's brow. The man was looking bumptious, quite different to when he was brought there. And if he was being properly guarded the fact was very little in evidence.

'And you first saw Fleece when?'

'I think it was twenty-eighth September.'

This was another perplexing point; it was Mrs Askham who was answering the questions. She'd also been crying, the Chief Constable was sure of it, her make-up was in a ghastly mess; and her tone, though clear, was low, so that he needed to lean forward to catch the responses. What had this London fellow been doing to her, the wealthiest woman in North Wales . . . ?

'What was his purpose in visiting you?'

'Reg.'

'A question of money?'

'No. Me.'

'He made a proposal?'

'If you can call it that.'

'And your son knew?'

'Yes. He was there.'

'What steps did you take as a result of the visit?'

'I consulted Clarence. He knew who I was.'

'What suggestion did Mr Stanley make?'

'None. There was nothing we could do.'

'So you agreed to the proposal?'

'I daren't not agree.'

'Did you know your son went looking for Kincaid?'

'Yes.'

'And what for?'

'Yes. A bribe. We were desperate.'

Presumably Gently was adding it together, and Evans too, from his intelligent attitude; but a freshly arrived Chief Constable was finding it difficult to pick up a cue. At last he drew out an amber cigar-holder, lit a cigar, and sat nursing his knee. The thing to do now was to think up an apology, something to smooth down the ruffled La Askham . . .

'And now we'll have your son's statement.'

Good lord, was there more of it? The Chief Constable touched his watch and looked meaningly at Evans. But no, there were no dissentients, this extension seemed understood. La Askham left the seat and her son took his place. And young Henry, he too was looking under the weather. He wasn't nearly as fierce as the C.C. remembered him. Altogether his appearance was decidedly hangdog, though with his driving habits he was no novice at these parties . . .

'Put in your own words what happened on Monday.'

'I . . . for certain reasons I wanted to meet Mr Kincaid. I'd heard from our housekeeper that he was staying in Caernarvon, so I went there to find him, and afterwards to Llanberis . . .'

Then, for the Chief Constable, the world abruptly ceased to turn. This was no simple statement: it was a full-dress confession. In horror he sat listening, with his cigar going cold on him; heard the damning words uttered in Henry Askham's halting voice.

'So I decided to wait there . . . in case I should see him . . .'

'Say where it was you waited, please.'

'On the cairn at the summit. I sat down because I felt dizzy . . .'

'What made you feel dizzy?'

'I've got a bad head for heights . . .'

And then the worst, or what was so near it that the worst must be inferred: a transparent evasion of a guilt that screamed aloud. A damned-good grilling must get the rest of it, of that there was no question. The case was made. Henry Askham was the self-confessed murderer of Fleece.

But the strangest part of it was the lack of emotion that accompanied this frightful revelation. Nobody appeared very much concerned, not even the droop-figured culprit. Gently was looking mildly bored; Evans had a distant, meditative expression; Mrs Askham was scarcely listening; and Kincaid was gawping at Mrs Askham. Did nobody care any longer about self-confessed murderers, even when millionaire-apparents, sons, and voiders of capital charges? It seemed they didn't. In fact, the atmosphere was wholly unaccountable. The C.C. felt like pinching himself to be assured that he didn't dream . . .

Now Mrs Askham had stirred herself.

'Then may I take it there will be no charge?'

That was the question. The C.C. found himself staring with open mouth at Gently. There *had* to be a charge, and yet . . . before Gently could speak, he knew it. It was part of the craziness he had stumbled into, the prevailing pattern of derangement.

'I don't think a charge will be necessary. But there is something I have to say to you.'

It was too much. He was reading them a lecture on the heinousness of false witness. Like two naughty children, they listened, the proud La Askham and her

220

fiery son, the one with submissive and downcast eyes, the other with a look that was near admiration. After this, the C.C. gave up. There could be no more attempt at intelligent appraisal. It mattered little that the Yard man was about to release his cherished prisoner; that was purely a formality. Open the cells. Let them all go.

And Kincaid:

'I feel greatly in your debt, Superintendent. Not only for clearing me of the charge. It goes much deeper than that.'

They were shaking hands; they all shook hands. It might have been an old chum's reunion. Then Kincaid offered his arm to Mrs Askham, and Mrs Askham laid her gloved hand on it . . .

When Gently returned to the office he found the C.C. seated behind the desk; with a perceptible stiffness in his bearing and a resolute gleam in his eye. He pointed to the seat of interrogation, sniffed and angled his moustache.

'Now,' he said. 'Perhaps a man can be told what's going on in his own division?'

Gently sat, feeling for his pipe.

'It's a long story,' he replied.

But it was simple too, for all stories were basically simple; the story of a rich man's enticement of a poor man's wife. Of the corrupting power of large possessions, of the cropping of dragon's teeth, and the ultimate destruction of a guilty one when no man pursued him. Simple and moral, if morals still lingered in a well-explained world. Simple anyway, like truth. A dramatic testimony for five players.

'Mrs Askham was very generous in filling in the minor detail.'

She had been; though wouldn't 'confessed' have been the word that best described it? Deliberately, never glancing at Kincaid, in her low, steady voice, she had rehearsed without excusing every incident of that long-ago. A confession, yes, and more: a revelation of herself. A picture of the woman as she was, pitilessly drawn for Kincaid to see. His blind devotion had made her honest, she'd felt compelled to render account. At least she would tender a rigid integrity to his unconditioning acceptance.

'She married Kincaid in the first place because she thought herself pregnant by Askham. They had had a brief affaire, very much a boss-employee relation. But after the marriage a change took place. Askham had taken a second look at her. He saw that her husband was deeply in love with her and it suggested that he'd thrown something away. He began to fall in love with her himself. Soon it was no longer enough for her to be his mistress. He grew jealous and possessive and wanted Paula entirely, he saw in Kincaid an interloper, a mere gesture to the proprieties.

'Towards the end of nineteen-thirty-six the situation became more critical, since Paula was really pregnant this time and there were reasons why Kincaid could not have been the father. A divorce was out of the question; it would have had business repercussions for Askham; and he wouldn't hear of an abortion even if that had been practicable. The only relief from the dilemma lay in the proposed Everest expedition, and this was languishing from lack of funds and want of an experienced leader. But Askham could provide it with both, and this he did, in strict secrecy. He did more. He suborned that leader in an effort to prevent Kincaid from ever returning. Fleece was serviceable, he was ambitious. It needed only a bribe to do the trick. The money was promised. Fleece agreed. Harry Askham had found a solution.

'Paula was naturally not informed of this second and criminal part of the arrangement. She knew only that Askham had put up the money and had influenced Fleece to lead the party. The bribe was substantial. It enabled Fleece to set up business on his return. His wife remembers him receiving the money and being delighted with himself about it.

'He was subtle, and from a professional standpoint one must admire the way he handled the job. He manoeuvred the assault, he worked his opening, and he brought back a story that was easy to believe in. It fitted Kincaid's character neatly, for he was just the man to continue alone. And it was accepted; people questioned Fleece's judgement, but his integrity went unchallenged. There remained a little matter of a lost climbing rope, but that passed unnoticed in the excitement of the moment.

'When news of the tragedy reached England, Askham acted without delay. It was not to be supposed that Paula was greatly stricken with grief. By an apparent miracle, her troubles were over and she could be united to her affluent lover, so she let him carry her off to Wales, where they were married by special licence. From Wales she never stirred until after the birth of her son Henry, and then she moved in circles remote from all who knew her as Mrs Kincaid. She had always been a person of refinement. She took care now to adapt herself to her environment. Askham married her for love, but he never had cause to regret it.

'Fleece returned and established his business and seemed content with his one bite at the cherry: in fact, with the guilt so evenly distributed, the prospect of blackmail was practically excluded. When Askham died the position was unaltered. Mrs Askham was his legitimate though harassed legatee. She had to fight for her rights. His brother Richard pressed her hard; but she won her case, and was safely installed in her millions.

'Then the impossible happened. The grave gave up its dead. From ten thousand miles and a dim memory Kincaid came stalking into the Asterbury. He had changed; he was hard to recognize; his manner was eccentric: and distrait; but from the moment he began his story Fleece, at all events, had no more doubt. Kincaid alone could know those facts and to know them branded the man as Kincaid. It was hardly surprising that Fleece lost his head and started a suit to discredit the intruder.

'He soon found it again, however; Fleece was a man with both eyes open. It may have been Kincaid's anxiety to trace his wife that revealed to Fleece his great opportunity. I imagine he'd kept an eye on the

Askhams. He knew just how vulnerable was Paula's position. And Kincaid could recognize her, that was a fair gamble, though it was highly unlikely that she would put it to the test. It was a situation that was tailor-made for blackmail. Fleece went to Wales and stated his demands.

'He wanted everything, her hand and her fortune. The small matter of his being married could be adjusted quite easily. For a year or two now he'd known that his wife had a lover, and his divorce was a formality which he put in hand directly. His position was unassailable and he revelled in his power. He made no bones about discussing the affair before her son. They were helpless. Their choice lay between Fleece and relative poverty. Any compromise they suggested he brushed insolently aside.

'That was the situation on Monday, with one significant development: Kincaid was in Caernarvon. He had been seen and recognized by Mrs Askham's housekeeper. His presence there then may have been fortuitous or it may have been contrived as a flick of the whip, but he was there, and that circumstance gave rise to a desperate plan. Henry Askham would seek him and confide to him the situation. He would offer him an unlimited bribe to declare himself an impostor. Askham sought for him in Caernarvon and was directed to Llanberis, and there discovered that Kincaid had bought sandwiches and had set off again up the Pass. Askham guessed, and guessed wrongly, that Kincaid had gone up Snowdon, and rather than miss him he went up also, taking what he judged to be the same track.

225

'You've heard his statement. He arrived at the summit a little ahead of the Everest Club party, and seeing them coming he decided to wait in case Kincaid should be among them. Because he was giddy he sat down on the cairn, which had the effect of concealing him, so that neither Heslington nor Fleece were aware of his presence when they arrived. But he saw them, especially Fleece. His hatred flared at the sight of him. To his tormented brain this was part of a plot, Fleece had come there to rendezvous with Kincaid. When Fleece went down to the edge and stood watching he was presumably on the look-out for his man, and Askham would have been less than human if a certain idea hadn't occurred to him.

'But there were two things against it. One was Askham's poor head for heights. I believe he would never have dared to go where Fleece was standing then. The other was the structure of the cairn, which, as you may know, is built of loose rock. It would have been physically impossible for Askham to have got down off it without making a noise and attracting Fleece's attention. And the distance between them was about forty-five feet, and Fleece was a powerful and heavily built man; so murder was out. I was convinced of that as soon as I had a chance to examine the place.

'What, then, happened? Askham was left with his original plan to pursue. Kincaid was coming, or so he thought, and with luck he might be intercepted. But by now Askham's nerves were so tattered that he was unfit for even this course, and after rising to his feet he lit a cigarette in an attempt to smooth them down.

Then he took a step forward, and made a clatter. Fleece turned to see Askham standing above him.

'The sequel is instructive: it was his sense of guilt and nothing else that did for Fleece. Askham had no intention of attacking him, nor could he have done so if he'd wished. But Fleece's guilt prevented him from seeing it. I imagine he had only one thought: here was a person who he'd driven to extremes, and who was about to act as he himself would have acted. The shock unnerved him. He gave a shout of dismay. He lost his balance, and with a scream toppled backwards.'

Gently broke off, his nice sense of timing warning him that here he should relight his pipe. His authority was felt, for neither the C.C. nor Evans unsettled the spell with a question. From outside came the patter of rain. It was beating insistently on the pavements below. Only just in time had they gone to the mountain, subpoenaing the sun to be a witness . . .

'Askham was petrified, but he knew he'd be a fool if he stopped there to explain matters. Forgetting his cigarette-case, which he'd dropped, he made tracks for Llanberis. At Trecastles he told his mother and they agreed between them to keep it quiet, but later he remembered the cigarette-case and the loss of it preyed on his mind. The case, of course, had been Kincaid's; it had a history of its own. It had been given him by his wife a short time before the expedition. But on the same day, which was his birthday, he'd learned something suspicious about his wife; there'd been a row, he'd returned the case, and she'd taken to using it as a gesture of defiance. Kincaid was disturbed when

I showed it him. It concealed a memory which he wanted kept concealed.

'However, the fact that it had been Kincaid's suggested a piece of embroidery to Askham. He knew by his own experience that people tended to remember Kincaid. So the next day he drove into Llanberis and reported to the police about seeing Kincaid, giving them the name of 'Basil Gwynne-Davies' and an address he'd noticed in Bangor. The result exceeded his expectations; he had intended only to confuse the inquiry. But on the evidence there was nothing we could do except to arrest Kincaid and charge him. And then immediately a fresh danger arose, since we were bound to investigate the antecedents of Kincaid, and so the threat which should have died with Fleece was revived in a second and more alarming form. The Askhams fled from Wales to London, where they consulted their friend, Mr Stanley. They conspired to obstruct what inquiry they could and, in Askham's case, to lay the ghost of Paula entirely.

'Again it was he who went one too many. I could credit Mrs Askham, and Stanley's obstructions only baffled me. But Henry's gambit I knew for a fake, it was much too obvious and convenient, and once I grasped how it tied in the case began to fall together. But Henry wasn't going to split, and showing motive wasn't enough. I had to know and prove before witnesses exactly what happened up there on Monday. So I put him through the reconstruction, which was the only course open to me. And it worked, I'm pleased to say. The rest was merely a matter of production.'

'So I noticed.' The C.C. was gruff after his long bout of silence. He looked away, tweaking his moustache with alternate jerkings of his face muscles. 'But, dash it all, there was a chance there . . . you needn't have sunk the lady's canoe. Once you were certain that it was an accident you might have given it the soft pedal.'

Gently nodded. 'I did think about it. Though she rated a reprimand. But then I saw it in a different way as I was coming down Snowdon.'

Evans said roundly: 'Kincaid, man,' as though he had suddenly solved a problem.

Gently nodded again. 'Yes, Kincaid, man. We owed him something. I thought his wife.'

He took the noon train for town after spending a Sunday morning with Evans, admiring Caernarvon, which was easy, and submitting to the Welshman's long post-mortem. Evans had lost, but he bore no grudge for it; he appeared to have forgotten his dimmed hopes of promotion. His object now was to study that case and to dwell on each aspect of the way Gently had handled it. He wanted to learn and he acknowledged his master. He acknowledged the insufficiency of his restless logic. He had seized on the secret that logic was not enough, and he wanted to be logically certain that he was reading it aright. He developed his ideas with a native fervour, and Gently responded to him generously.

At the police station they met the Chief Constable again: another man who had been indulging in meditations on Kincaid. He succeeded in cornering Gently in the superintendent's office, where after some introductory compliments he came down to the business near to him.

'You know, I can't help thinking that our man was a bit simple. Damn it, he might have waited a day before hanging a charge on Kincaid.'

Poor Evans. Gently was glad that the office door was closed between them. He paused before returning an answer and raised his brows in surprised dissent.

'Our Assistant Commissioner was convinced we had a case against Kincaid.'

'Oh, was he?' The C.C.'s tone sounded deferential but doubting. 'All the same, it was rather hasty. He showed a lack of judgement, I thought. It doesn't do our name any good to go throwing capital charges around.'

'In principle, of course.' Gently conceded the point ungraciously. 'But in the circumstances we felt your man acted properly and with intelligence. Kincaid's apprehension was necessary: he appeared to have had a powerful motive for murder. He was also in funds and he had no ties. He might have disappeared at any moment.'

'I see your point.' The C.C. thought about it. He continued to look unenthusiastic. 'Perhaps I'm being wise after the event, but you must admit I have some grounds for it.'

'You're doing less than justice to Evans.'

'Oh no. I've always thought him a good man.'

'He's more than that.' Gently took a plunge. 'We could use him in Whitehall if you'd agree to his transfer.'

'If I agree—!' The C.C. was startled. 'Good heavens no. I'll hear of nothing like that.'

'He's the sort we need. I can vouch for him personally.'

'No, Gently. We can't let you pinch our Evanses.'

But now he looked pleased. He took a turn up the office.

'It's like this,' he said abruptly. 'Owens here is retiring. It's been a toss-up whether we promote Evans or move in the superintendent from Bangor. But you've seen something of Evans and you seem to think him a deserving customer—'

'I have to agree with our Assistant Commissioner.'

'Exactly. And in view of his opinion . . .'

Gently was still chuckling over that interview when his train pulled away from Menai, leaving Evans, a waving figure, standing alone at the platform's end. Then he settled to his papers: 'Kincaid . . . Dramatic Move . . . Release'; but by Penmaen-mawr he'd fallen asleep, with the vestige of a smile still lining his face.

For how else could one look at the Kincaid affair? From first to last, it had been a preposterous business.

Brundall, 1959–60